FIRSTBORN

Book 1 of
The Legacy Series

RYAN ATTARD

Firstborn
Ryan Attard

Copyright © 2013 by Ryan Attard. All rights reserved. This is a work of fiction. Any resemblance to actual persons living or dead, businesses, events or locales is purely coincidental. Reproduction in whole or part of this publication without express written consent is strictly prohibited.

Visit:
Ryanattard.com

For my wonderful family for their never-ending support.
For my friend and editor Roberta.
For my dedicated fans and readers - thank you.

Chapter 1

It was probably the black trench coat I wore despite the afternoon sun, or the twin guns strapped to my thighs, like an action movie hero, or the short sword handle occasionally poking out from under my coat.

Any of these could have been why everyone averted their eyes as I hurriedly walked down the streets of my hometown in the La Fortunata district, Eureka. I get the irony, too. There was nothing fortunate about the constant appearance of supernatural creatures or the fear that permeates the air every minute of every day around here.

My name is Erik Ashendale, wizard extraordinaire, and I'm perfectly comfortable with the sideways glances.

Hell, they all knew what I did for a living. They all poked their heads into my office window, hoping to catch a glimpse of me performing a ritual which summoned forth some ancient demonic entity, or the other crap they see on TV. All they saw was my extensive collection of trinkets and, occasionally, my cat licking itself.

To be fair, that would horrify anyone.

I arrived at my destination, a narrow street in the quiet part of town. Or at least it was quiet before today's events.

Police cruisers were piled in front of the entrance of the local elementary school, creating a thick black and blue wall on an otherwise grey road. Uniformed officers were bent over open car doors or kneeling behind their vehicles, their pistols steady in their hands, while others held shotguns, poking from beneath cover, and aimed squarely at the building.

"You're late."

I turned around and came face-to-face with a young police officer in plainclothes. "Fashionably so," I replied.

Detective Roland March shifted his stance, a sign he was under stress, and fumbled in his jacket pocket for a pack of cigarettes.

"Well, now you're here. That's good." He extracted a lighter and struck it three times before a small flame appeared. It took him another couple of tries to light the cancer stick. "I didn't know who else to call. The chief is on my ass and I'm lost out here. We've shot at them but bullets don't seem to affect them." Roland's voice was shaking now.

"And," he continued, his eyes now wide open, "they weren't human. I swear, Erik, they looked like giant walking lizards. No one will admit to it of course, but we all saw it. Looked like they belonged in a cheap sci-fi flick." He sucked deeply on his cigarette and did his best to hide his nerves from other officers nearby.

"Lizards?" I asked.

This wasn't the first time the law needed my help with some extraordinary case. Usually my job consisted of looking at cadavers and figuring out how they were ripped in two, while the coroner sits at the back denying everything not found in textbooks.

But sometimes, my job gets a little more exciting.

"Long necks, elongated snouts, tail thrashing about? Like an iguana on steroids?" I asked.

"Yes!" Roland yelped. "Exactly like that. There are at least five of them in there." The cigarette was half gone by now.

I smiled happily, much to Roland's chagrin. "Lizardmen," I said. "You found lizardmen. They're like the Big Foot of supernatural zoology. It's been decades since the last documented sighting."

I couldn't keep the glee out of my voice. Everyone is a geek about something. There are people who are completely obsessed with *Star Wars*, or comic book characters. Heck, I even knew a guy in elementary school who just wouldn't shut up about airplanes.

Liking my job is probably what keeps me sane.

"I don't care what they are or how long it's been since someone saw them," Roland hissed angrily. "Just tell me how to kill them. There are kids in there." He lit a second cigarette.

"You guys can't handle them," I replied. "Only I can.

With my… um… methods."

Roland leaned in close. "You mean magic, right?"

I wrinkled my nose against the foul smell of his breath. "Yes, magic."

Roland is perhaps the only cop who knows about the existence of magic. We've known each other for a couple of years now, ever since I saved him from a newly turned vampire when he was still a beat cop. The guy thought he was dealing with some kid hopped up on PCP. I happened to be wondering by and saved the young officer. About year ago he got promoted to detective and kept hiring me as a 'consultant' every time he ran into something cuffs and bullets couldn't handle.

I yanked the half-finished cigarette out of his mouth and channeled my magic through it. The amber glowed until the whole thing burst into flames.

"Hey, I wasn't done with that!"

"Yes, you were. Smoking too much of this stuff will get you killed. And I need this gig. I got bills to pay." I walked with him towards the police cars.

"So, what's the plan?" he asked quietly.

"You get rid of every camera around here. I'll go in and do my thing. When I'm done, I'll call you. Then you'll collect the kids and everybody will live happily ever after."

"You wanna go in alone?"

"Yeah. If any of you go in, you'll just be providing them with a free lunch. You guys aren't suited for this type of threat," I said grimly. "You'll only slow me down and I can't babysit anyone. Not when there are innocent lives involved."

I was being harsh, but sometimes you have to be direct to get your point across, and this was the language that most cops understood.

Roland raised his hands. "Fine. I'm not gonna argue. I'll say you're a negotiator or something. Just call me the second it's safe for my officers to go in that place. And Erik-"

"Yeah?"

"Don't screw up."

I smirked. "When have I ever?"

Before Roland could retort back with some very true accounts of my behavior around his crime scenes, I made my way to the front door of the school.

I un-holstered my guns, a pair of identical Berettas, and took a deep breath. My sister was going to be so jealous when she heard about this. She might even chew my head off for not capturing one alive.

After a few seconds of smiling like an idiot and pushing away the slowly building anxiety, I felt ready to confront the horrors that had the entire police force cowering in their boots.

"Let's go negotiate."

Chapter 2

I may have magical powers, and I may make a living fighting off monsters, but I am still human. And every human has a reason to fear the dark.

I knew they were there; I could feel their creepy lizard eyes on me. Of course, they were observing me. They were natural hunters.

The first indication was a slither. It always starts with a slither, a movement in your peripheral vision and the whisper of a shadow. Then, once you look closely enough, the shadow grows into a nightmare.

There were two of them, attached to the walls like the most bizarre ornaments in existence. Their claws were spayed for a good grip on the flat surface, their long, thin bodies held flat with only the tail moving like a lazy rudder. Their necks were unnaturally long for lizards and made them look like miniature theropods.

Really bizarre, not-so-herbivorous theropods.

I couldn't see them so much as feel their presence. My

eyes could only pick out jerks of movements and the occasional yellow eye-shine. The entire corridor was coated in tangible darkness. I recognized the telltale signs of magic and knew someone other than the non-sentient lizardmen must have cast this spell. My mind had already displayed the red flags, the little hints of foul play. But it would all have to wait.

I channeled my magic into my guns and there was silence no more. My powers enhanced the bullets, leaving little red streaks of light in their wake. It was a preemptive strike, meant to break up the formation. Surely enough, both creatures scurried about, hissing like crazy.

I focused on one, trailing bullets behind it. The hiss became a croak, confirming that at least one of my shots had met its target. I saw something thrashing about and fired off a couple more rounds. Better safe than sorry when it comes to giant flesh eating lizards.

I stopped firing and focused my eyes.

A tail. That damn lizardman shed its tail.

I sensed the owner coming back at me. In a practiced movement I holstered the guns and reached under my coat, pulling out Djinn, my magical short sword. My magic reacted with it, making the blade glow azure, and the lizardman veered to one side. I fully extracted the weapon and held it aloft. It was about half a meter in length, with a double-edged blade and a leather-wrapped hilt. My finger slid in its crossguard, a thick ring in between the blade and the handle. The short sword emitted blue light like a glow stick.

I felt both lizardmen cower away from the light. That would explain the darkness magic. It was daylight outside, and having monsters which are afraid of sunlight wasn't very useful.

Not unless you cast a spell specifically designed to dissipate light and turn the area pitch black. But as I said, lizardmen can't cast magic.

What the hell was going on here?

I poured magic into the weapon and sliced the air. Energy streaked from the weapon in a crescent shape towards the first lizardman. It let out a scream and fell silent. Without missing a beat, I spun and stabbed. Djinn's blade elongated, growing four times its usual size until, like a spear, it impaled the second lizardman on the other side of the corridor.

I smiled, relishing in my victory. I mean, come on, if waving around a glowing magic sword and battling giant lizards doesn't get you going, you're dead inside.

But in that moment, that little microsecond where I let my guard drop, was when the third lizardman emerged.

My senses picked it up too late. I felt a blow on my right side and was knocked through a door and into a vacant classroom. The monster, erect on two legs, hissed furiously and stomped after me. I groped for Djinn and found nothing.

"Crap, crap, crap, crap," I cursed, each word louder than the one before it.

I pulled out my pistols and started firing at the lizardman. The last thing I saw was its giant shadow looming over me. I closed my eyes and kept on pulling triggers until my fingers ached and the guns clicked empty.

There was a ringing in my ears, like when you suddenly turn off a really loud stereo and all you hear is that faint, high-pitched sound. Once my ears adjusted, there was complete silence.

I opened my eyes and saw a dead lizardman splayed on the ground, its head resting comfortably between my legs.

"That went well," I muttered, partially in sarcasm, as I retrieved Djinn. A series of deep breaths helped my racing heartbeat regain its normal tempo. I made it back to the pitch-black corridor, in the middle of darkness.

There are many ways to undo a spell. A subtle and cunning magician would take some time to study the mechanics and energy flow and then find the right component to remove.

But I am neither subtle nor cunning—I like blowing shit up.

With Djinn held high I poured my magic into it, turning its blue glow into painful white light. After a few seconds it became a hot, searing, smiting supernova that pushed back against the swallowing darkness. Atmospheric pressure dipped and my ears popped.

And then, it was over.

Natural light hit the walls, revealing a very mediocre paint job. I heard things that had been dulled out before, like the chirping of birds, the tense orders from the police officers outside, and the muffled whimpering of children. Following the latter sound, I came to a plain wooden door and placed one hand on it.

I concentrated on the flow of energy behind the door. Huddled in a corner were a bunch of tiny energy bundles: the children, presumably. Directly in front of the door, as if it were some grotesque bouncer, was a jagged and sharp energy signature vibrating at an erratic pace and swirling in unnatural patterns. Its shape, color, and texture were completely different from that of the children.

This was the aura of a lizardman.

I willed my eyes open again. It wasn't a good idea to fight in front of those kids. If I made a single error they would end up suffering and that was unacceptable in my book.

Instead, I calculated the position of the monster and pointed Djinn at where I assumed its chest would be. I placed the sword's tip on the cheap, wooden door and channeled my magic once more.

The azure blade shot through the door and embedded itself inside the lizardman's sternum, throwing it across the room, dead and immovable.

I opened the door and sheathed my sword.

Suddenly, the air in front of me popped and the last of the lizardmen materialized out of thin air. I froze and stared at it, eyes wide open.

This one was clearly different from the others.

Its hide was a different shade of gray, lighter and milkier. Its eyes glowed yellow and were shaped like a cat's rather than a reptile's. It had slender limbs lined with wiry muscles. Its tail was shorter and stouter, as if its owner had evolved beyond the purpose of needing a tail. The snout was considerably shorter, like its neck.

But the real dangers were those claws. The unusually straight, sharp claws it bore on each hand were serrated on one side.

Nature had already given lizardmen everything they needed to survive—the claws, the teeth, the thick skin. There simply was no need to evolve. To my knowledge, none ever had serrated claws or any of the features that this particular specimen bore.

The lizardman flicked its thumb and forefinger claws against each other. It honestly reminded me of someone waiting impatiently. It looked disturbingly human and those intelligent eyes spoke of evolution beyond that of its cousins.

It dawned on me that those serrations were self-inflicted. It had found a way to improve what nature had given it—just like a human being.

The monster's crocodile smile widened as it plunged one clawed hand into my chest.

And as I fell to my knees and onto the ground, I thought, *Did that giant gecko just chuckle at me?*

I did not die.

Yeah, I fell face forwards in a pool of my own blood—but I did not die.

Call it a curse or whatever, but I guess my special condition has got its advantages at times. You see, I'm not exactly what you might call a generic wizard. My sister and I were born under a curse. I don't really get most of it, but here's the gist. She got the brains of a genius but lacks the raw magical power to do much. She can still kick some ass, but that's my major. I got raw energy, tons of it. Problem is, it's too much for me to handle.

So, yeah, I'm a wizard who can't use magic. Pretty useless, right?

Well, that's not completely true. I can use magic if I channel it through something, like a gun or a sword. Otherwise, there's a chance my own powers could disintegrate me. Not a pretty picture.

There is, however, one very sweet upside to my condition.

"Hey, ugly," I rasped. Both guns were in my hands and I found the strength to get up and aim.

The lizardman spun, poised to attack. I squeezed both triggers at an inhuman pace, forcing the guns to spit magically enhanced lead at a rate that no human could ever achieve. The shrapnel tore the lizardman's body to shreds. I looked down and hoped that I wouldn't see a gaping hole in my chest. I felt my magic converge around the wound and heal it almost instantly.

Detective March burst into the room seconds later, flooding it with SWAT officers.

"Nice job, er… holy shit," Roland exclaimed as he pointed at my guns.

The barrels had completely melted and molten steel was dripping down like water.

"How the hell?" I remarked as I emptied any bullets from the guns and tentatively pulled their triggers to check the mechanism.

As I did so, both pistols simply exploded into a million pieces, leaving me standing there with nothing but a pair of very useless grips. I felt like a cartoon character after a bomb goes off in their face.

Police officers shook their heads in disbelief and murmured between themselves. I glanced at the nearest police officer, a blonde female with an intense look.

"I'm too hot to handle," I said, waving the actual pistol handles around. "Get it?"

She gave me a look as if I was a fly she had found in her salad.

It was Roland's turn to shake his head. "Don't bother. Every single cop in this town has heard stories about you," he said, condescendingly patting me on the back.

Oh great, now the guy gets to patronize me.

"All good stories, I hope."

"Good stories, yes. Mostly funny ones. You never look good in any of them," he said, no longer trying to hide his amusement.

I sighed. "Then they're probably true."

Chapter 3

"Ugh, what a day."

I slumped on my couch and cracked my stiff neck. It was hot as hell this time of the year. Maybe I should invest in an air conditioner, not that I could afford one. All I had was a ceiling fan lazily spinning around, but it felt more like a blowdryer. I looked at the remains of my guns, slumped carelessly on the coffee table and sighed.

Nope, no air conditioner for Erik.

Maybe I could sell something, though I doubt I'd find anyone with my interests. Both sides of the room were littered with cabinets and wardrobes full of occult ornaments and artifacts, some of them gimmicks to sell an image, others the real thing.

There was a cheap, wooden desk at the far end of one wall. It looked like an antique. I got it at a pawn shop for a hundred. Not that I had any real use for it.

Most of its surface was littered with Chinese takeout cartons and empty soda cans. There were some metallic parts on one side. Those belonged to the jukebox. The ancient music player had been left here when I'd gotten the place, and I loved that thing. It had a collection of records that I never got tired of listening to. Anything from sixties jazz, to Elvis albums, and even a few MC Hammer vinyls.

Maybe I should put something on and doze off. I had found that naps were a good cure for dealing with the trauma of having a giant lizard impale you.

Even thinking about it made me uneasy; an evolved lizardman. How the hell was that possible? Someone was messing with the natural order of things. Lizardmen don't just appear and terrorize schools. Someone surely must have used magic to mutate that monster, someone that I would probably encounter again and would have to stop.

And most likely not get paid for it.

I closed my eyes.

My nap lasted exactly five seconds.

I felt a ball of fur settle on my chest. I snapped wide awake and swung off the couch, hitting my leg on the coffee table and falling face forward onto the rug beneath.

"Ow," I heard myself moan pathetically. Not one of my finest moments.

Amaymon sat on the coffee table, chuckling. The black American shorthair cat flicked its tail, clearly enjoying watching the clumsy human trip over him.

"Dammit, Amaymon," I said as I nursed a bump on my head. "I told you to stop doing that."

"And I told you I will not stop as long as you keep reacting like a frightened eight-year-old girl."

Amaymon talks.

He's a talking cat. A very annoying talking cat.

Don't be fooled, he's not all cuddles. Amaymon is a demon, and a very unique one at that. He belongs to a very old branch of demons, those that existed in Hell way before the first humans learned to rub two sticks together for fire. He was also an elemental, governing anything to do with earth.

A few centuries ago he was the second in command in Hell, right under the Emperor. He led demon armies and waged war like a Viking on a mission.

Right until he rubbed my family off the wrong way. They captured him, turned him into a cat, locked away all of his powers into an amulet and eventually made him into a little, kitty-shaped paperweight.

Now, he spends his time doing cat-like things such as sleeping all day, licking himself and giving me disapproving looks.

Except his looks come with a commentary.

"And you broke your guns again I see. That's the second time this month, isn't it?" He played around with the parts, rubbing his claws against them.

I made it to the kitchen and grabbed a soda can from the fridge.

"Oh God, not another lecture from the damn cat," I moaned as I pressed the soda can against my forehead.

"Stop using regular junk as channels. Breaking stuff is not in your best interest. You're already behind on your bills," Amaymon continued, completely ignoring my complaint.

"It was a critical situation," I replied weakly.

"Critical, my tail."

"Amaymon, you're an immortal demon trapped in a cat's body. Are you really gonna bitch about money?"

"Yes," he replied promptly. "If you starve to death no one can buy my food. I mean, I could always eat you after you're dead but, bleh. I doubt you'd have any nutritional value. Not to mention a complete lack of taste." He chuckled at his own pun.

"I'm so glad you draw the line at cannibalism," I said.

"Dude, you gotta be of the same species for it to be cannibalism."

It's always a relief to know you're taken care of after you pass away.

"By the way, the mechanic called," he said. "Your car in still in the shop. He's gonna need a few more days to fix that kind of damage."

"Oh, great," I said sarcastically. I popped the can open and gulped the cool drink inside.

Amaymon hopped on my lap. "You're having one of those *I hate my life* moments, aren't you?"

"Uh huh."

"Hey, I can start munching on you right now if you want," he offered. "Get an early start."

I frowned at the cat and put my soda can down. Lifting the cat by its collar, I dragged him all the way to a corner in the office where a bowl was filled with catnip.

"Munch on that," I said, dropping him.

He began to savagely devour the contents of the bowl,

when his ears twitched. "Someone's coming."

Amaymon was probably the most reliable home security system, if you were willing to put up with sarcasm. I hadn't even put the *open* sign up yet. Was the monster population in Eureka that bad? I'm almost certain people don't show up at my doorstep because of my charming personality.

Amaymon hissed. That was generally a bad sign.

"Let's see what the universe is plaguing me with now," I said, smiling at my own wit.

I opened the door and was greeted by a short, young girl dressed in an olive-green, Victorian-style suit complete with an ascot and cloak. Her platinum-blonde hair gleamed in the afternoon sun and her skin seemed to glisten. Penetrating green eyes matched my own color, but hers burned with an intensity that seemed to weigh your soul and then judge accordingly.

Behind her stood a very tall and lanky man dressed in a traditional butler's suit. His long wavy hair was pulled back into a ponytail, held firm with a midnight-blue ribbon. His most striking features were his eyes. They matched Amaymon's: golden orbs with black slits. He grinned, revealing a set of pointed, serrated teeth, the kind you would expect to see on a shark. Behind them, a pair of bodyguards stood still, like statues. They wore the typical *Men in Black* outfits, complete with the iconic dark shades.

My sister broke the increasingly awkward silence. "Hello, brother."

I looked up towards the clear blue sky and sighed.

"Good one, universe."

Chapter 4

She didn't reply. Or nod, or glare or show any reaction that a normal human being would for that matter.

Instead, my fraternal twin sister simply strode in past me and into my office, as if she owned the damn place. Guess it's hard to be considerate of other people when you've lived like a queen your entire life.

I shut the door and put on my best fake smile.

"Hi, Gil. It's been too long. How are you doing? Can I get you anything? Perhaps something to go."

They say siblings fight, but whoever they were have clearly never been a part of my family. To say Gil and I have a strained relationship was like saying Hitler may have disliked Jews.

After our psychotic father tried to kill us, she decided to continue the family tradition of obscure magic, capturing monsters and experimenting with some very dark stuff. I guess that's what Warlocks did. Our entire family was born to a line of Warlocks and I guessed Gil wanted to carry on the family tradition.

We had an argument about that.

It did not go well.

I ended up going my own separate way and renouncing my Warlock heritage, reverting back to the status of a wizard.

That way I slept better at night.

Gil sat on the couch next to the cat. Like royalty, her poise and posture were impeccable—the way she crossed her hands in her lap and sat upright, advertising her aristocratic upbringing.

She sighed and her lip trembled. Whatever she was here for made her uncomfortable, much to my pleasure.

"I have a big problem, Erik."

"That's next door. We're small-to-medium problems here."

Amaymon let out a soft chuckle. Gil wasn't impressed. Sometimes I think I was the one who got all the sense of humor in the family.

"The mansion's creatures have escaped," she said seriously.

I blinked a couple of times.

"Escaped?" I asked, all notion of humor gone from my voice.

"Yes. All gone."

"That's not good."

"Glad you're finally catching on," she replied.

Magic users are divided in one of three categories. First, you had the practitioners or adepts, the guys who could pull a spell or two, but were usually the textbook magicians.

Then you had wizards. Those guys had major power and could use every spell out there, as long as they practiced enough and had enough juice to back it up.

Finally, the Specialists. Those guys were nuclear-powered in comparison to the others, but could only use one category of magic. Warlocks fell under this category.

My family have always been Warlocks. We even had a creepy mansion in the middle of the forest, which was very appropriate considering Warlocks were the black sheep of the magical community. Beneath the Ashendale manor was a sub-basement which housed some of our… experiments.

Yeah, it creeps me out too.

The only thing worse than having those things down there imprisoned was having them running free. There were some horrors which could easily destroy life as we know it; a Crocatoan virus which may or may not have been the real cause of the Black Plague, an ancient forest spirit that could render a city as large as New York into a giant, uninhabitable forest, and a particularly ambitious Skinwalker who had the bright idea to kill a president and impersonate him. Only flaw was that the president had already been reported dead in the media.

But you get the idea. Heck, I wouldn't be surprised if Cthulhu and Lord Voldemort were locked up down there.

"How did they escape?" I asked.

Gil took a moment before answering. "It's unlikely that any of the monsters down there managed to open the gates themselves. Our security systems were breached by someone who is intimately familiar with them. Whoever it was simply picked the locks open and disabled all the security, magical or otherwise, before simply walking out the front door. They even managed to hack into two of our bank accounts. Luckily, I keep sixteen open at all times and in different locations. But I digress."

She bore her green eyes into mine with an intensity that made my skin crawl.

"It seems we have a traitor in our midst," she said, her voice quivering slightly with carefully controlled rage. My sister didn't take losing all that well.

"A traitor?" I echoed.

"Why do you think she's traveling with extras from *Men in Black* and her watchdog following her around?" Amaymon interjected.

The butler grinned. "I thought the cat got your tongue, brother."

Meet Mephisto; butler, Gil's familiar and Amaymon's brother. He's an air elemental and, just to prove that demons have no sense of irony, his animal form was of a large, black dog.

"Bite me, jackass," Amaymon replied with a hiss.

Mephisto's form shimmered and a black canine the size of a small bear bared its fangs at the cat. "Gladly."

"Enough, Mephistopheles," Gil ordered. "Behave yourself."

The dog transformed again and the butler took a step back, sulking.

"So, what's with the suits?" I asked Gil as I pointed at the two bodyguards. The more I looked at them, the more I realized something was off.

For one thing, there was a faint emission of light from their skin. I concentrated harder, forcing my eyes to look beyond their physical bodies and at their magical forms. There was a minute explosion of light before my eyes started burning. I caught a faint glimpse of wings and pure white feathers.

"Angels?"

It wasn't a question so much as a statement of how dumb my sister could be at times. You do not mess around with angels, or demons for that matter. Sure, their dimensions of Heaven and Hell were of opposite sides of our own dimension, but we do not interfere, or even communicate for that matter.

Those guys have been at war since the beginning of time. If that war moved to our reality, chances were all of us would end up as collateral damage.

"Since when do you employ angels?" I snarled.

"Calm down, Erik. There is an explanation," Gil replied.

"Better be a damn good one. You know as well as I do that those things can't be controlled."

Angels weren't exactly what they're cut out to be. I mean, sure, some lit up and brought joy to the kids, but they were ruthless soldiers, first and foremost. They smote whoever and whatever they considered impure.

And former Warlocks with no qualms about toeing the line tended to be at the top of their hit lists.

"Is there an apocalypse I should know about?" Amaymon asked.

I wish he was kidding. When angels come over, it meant something big was about to happen.

"These angels are merely on loan from a higher power. I had to invoke some assistance in order to deal with another issue," Gil replied.

I shrugged. "Whatever mess you got yourself into is not my problem." I jabbed an accusing finger at her. "And don't come whining to me when this comes back to bite you in the ass."

"I will deal with my own problems. In the meantime, I have a job for you," she said as she rummaged in her coat. She pulled out a thick roll of bills and set it of the coffee table. "This is a down payment for the capture of a Behemoth-type demon. My resources are spread too thin and this monster will be troublesome. Do you accept?"

I barely heard what she said. I was too busy drooling over the cash.

"Yes," I heard myself say.

"Behemoths tend to possess and mutate animals. Maybe you could check out the park or an animal shelter," Amaymon said.

"Yeah."

Gil rose. "You have your mission, brother: search and destroy. Get rid of that Behemoth demon."

Her voice was stone cold and authoritative. I've always wanted a voice like that. Maybe if I had I could finally get the cat to stop scratching at every stick of furniture around here.

Gil and her entourage left without another word.

Amaymon was the first to break the silence after they left. "A traitor?" he scoffed. "Like that place needs any more drama and back-stabbing."

I produced a fresh soda can, sat down next to him and drank heartily.

I remembered visiting our zoo as part of my training when we were kids. Gil was right. This stank of foul play.

You can't just walk up into the Ashendale mansion. The whole place was stronghold of magic. Dozens of barriers subconsciously repelled any hikers that showed up while a team of wizard mercenaries protected the mansion on a twenty-four hour watch. That place was more secure than Fort Knox and the Pentagon put together.

The zoo was located in the basement, two floors below ground. Everyone visiting had to go through a series of checks where everyone, family members included, faced a retinal scan, hand-scanner, voice recognition scans, and squeezed a couple of blood droplets into a hole.

Not exactly a vacation spot.

And if all that failed, there was Mephisto. Gil's familiar was a hunter. If unleashed, he could track whatever disturbance there was and, depending on his mood, he would either kill and then rip the body apart, or vice-versa. Honestly, I would prefer being shot and burned by the ninja wizards.

"Yeah. But it does raise the question," I said. "How did they get out? I mean, I grew up there and even I doubt even I could have made it out. The only way those monsters could have escaped is with a map and a tour guide."

"Agreed," said the cat. "By the way, what's up with you? You're all jumpy and stuff."

"What?"

Amaymon flicked his tail in annoyance. "Dude, I'm a demon, and despite being in the same room as two angels, I wasn't the one lashing out."

"I didn't lash out."

"Okay, you had a hissy fit, whatever you wanna call it," he said dismissively. "Just tell me what happened at the school that got you all grouchy."

So, I told him. I gave him every single detail, including the mutated lizardman that poked an extra hole in me.

"Yeah, that sounds just about right," he said. "What you described sounds a lot like a forced mutation. Someone got hold of a pack of lizardmen and played around with their genetics. Question is, why?"

I shrugged.

"Erik, who do the police call when something weird happens in this town?"

"Me," I replied.

"Exactly," he said. "What if whoever this was has a bone to pick with you?"

"Huh?"

"Think about it. Is there any reason why a bunch of monsters would attack a school?" His eyes poured into mine.

"They didn't kill the kids and never touched the officers. They were waiting for someone to enter the school, and the only person in this town crazy enough to do so is you. That whole thing was a setup."

"But if someone's got beef with me, why not just come at me directly?"

"Erik, you're nearly immortal. You heal instantly and your magical capacity rivals that of hardcore demons. Whoever it was didn't want a clean fight."

I felt the headache come back. "So, what do I do now?"

Amaymon chuckled. "What you always do. Rub people the wrong way and hope you don't bite the big one."

"Great," I muttered.

"You know, I could always help out," he said hopefully. "Especially if I had some power."

Amaymon's demon power is sealed inside a ruby pendant I wear around my neck at all times. If I put it on his collar and give him back his power, Amaymon could go back to his former badass self. He was handy in a pinch, but there was a huge chance he would destroy everything else in the process.

The guy just loved chaos and destruction.

"Not yet," I said. "I'll call you if I need backup."

Amaymon hissed. "Man, sometimes you can be a real-"

I raised an eyebrow at him challengingly.

"Mew," he finished.

I reached down and scratched his chin. "Clean up in here will you, kitty cat?"

"You know I hate that nickname," he replied as he purred.

I stood up and put on my coat and equipment. Time to go back to work.

"Don't burn the place down, okay?" I called to the cat.

"No promises."

Chapter 5

"What. Did you. Do?"

Bobby glared at me from behind the counter and looked at the remnants of my guns with something close to tears.

"Nothing," I replied, doing my best to avoid eye contact with him.

The wizened old blacksmith put his hands on his hips and looked just like a headmaster berating a student. "You were up to your mumbo-jumbo thing, weren't you?"

Well, at least he didn't call it voodoo this time. I suppose that was an improvement from the rest of the idiots around here.

"It's called work, Bobby." His look didn't change. "Okay yeah," I finally said in surrender. "The mumbo-jumbo."

The old man shook his head in disapproval. "That's the last time I give you new guns. From now on you get the bootlegs."

"That's what you said last time."

"And I damn well mean it this time, boy."

Bobby was a genius with guns. He could take an inch of rusting iron and two ounces of copper and whip up a fully functional machine gun. He was a true artist and those guys always got too attached to their work. And I didn't score any points by coming in nearly twice a month, dumping the scraps of old guns and asking for replacements.

Bobby gave me one last look of disapproval and went over to his workbench. "Here's your new piece."

He placed a flintlock on the bench. It had been refurbished with modern parts and had a box magazine locked in place in front of the trigger guard.

I blinked twice at Bobby. "Seriously?"

Bobby nodded.

"What the hell is that thing?" My voice was more high-pitched than usual.

Bobby cocked an eyebrow. "It's a heavily modified flintlock. This thing right here is the sturdiest gun in the whole store. It's custom-built for durability, so you can use it for whatever it is you do. That box mag takes shotgun rounds, so unless you're going up against an elephant, you're fine."

I cocked an eyebrow at the weapon.

"It's all I got left, boy. Take it or leave it," Bobby said in his headmaster voice again.

I snatched up the gun. "Thanks, Bobby," I said sincerely, before heading out.

***

For a giant, monstrous demon that possesses and deforms

animals, the Behemoth was damn hard to find.

I had spent an entire afternoon going from one animal shelter to another, but still no sign of the demon. I mean seriously, how hard could it be to find a couple of monsters that looked like they came right out of *Jumanji*?

I was just about to give up and head home. Maybe I could resume the hunt tomorrow, right after I found a suitable holster for the flintlock. The chunky gun hung inside the waistband of my trousers, making me look like an extra from *Pirates of the Caribbean*.

I kept fidgeting with it, trying to somehow find a comfortable position when I walked past the park and caught sight of a sign that read *zoo*. I was supposed to check that place out but kept putting it off. I tended to avoid places with kids everywhere and tired out parents glaring at them.

Ah screw it, I thought after a pause.

I walked in, ignoring all the looks, and bought a ticket. I may have even flirted with the receptionist.

Five minutes later I was walking down the animal exhibits alone.

And there it was.

The elephant exhibit was a late entry to the zoo. It was the largest exhibit and farthest from the entrance. Strangely enough it wasn't the most popular exhibit and only a few people were around. Maybe it was the thirty minute walk from the reception to the elephant place.

At the very back of the herd, completely on its own, was the possessed monster.

It was twice the size of a regular elephant and way too bizarre.

Its body slumped downwards like a mammoth's and its legs were not the usual trunk-shaped paws, but rather lupine legs with thick, obsidian claws. Its ears were thick black sails that waved to and fro, while reindeer horns branched outwards where the tusks on a normal elephant should be. The thick enamel forked outwards like a tree, creating an entire bush of sharp spikes around the monster's face. Its trunk was muscular and stocky, and instead of nostrils a pair of leaf-shaped blades emerged, promising a whole new world of pain.

The entire monster was covered in long fur that was darker than black.

It aimed a bloodshot red eye at me and I felt my knees buckling slightly.

"Holy crap."

My quip triggered a chain reaction.

The Behemoth reared on two legs and let out a bellow, sending everyone but me running out of the exhibit. I reached for the gun and pointed it at the monster.

Well, Bobby did say it could kill anything up to an elephant. Let's see if the new toy was up to the challenge.

A scream emanated throughout the now-empty exhibit. A kid was clutching a stuffed giraffe and began trembling as he and the monster made eye contact.

Chapter 6

My plan was simple: yell as loud as possible so the giant Behemoth-possessed elephant would attack me, instead of the helpless little boy.

Very heroic, right?

But then the plan actually worked and the monster turned its attention towards me. My screams were not part of the plan. From then onwards it was all improvisation, or as I call it, the *don't-get-yourself-killed* plan.

Which sounded easy enough until the Behemoth swiped its trunk at me.

I heard the blades whistle by, missing my hairline by a breeze. Instead, they met the gravel and left a pair of very deep grooves.

Years of fighting monsters had its advantages. My body reacted and I fired at its exposed neck. The gun buckled in my hand. The creature roared but seemed otherwise unaffected. The trunk swung again, this time closer to the mark. I ducked under the scything blades, barely avoiding being beheaded.

Suddenly, it charged.

Those white tusks it had on each side jutted at me. I crouched into a roll and caught the impact on my side. The momentum of the blow sent me flying into a wall. I felt ribs break, and my breathing became heavy and very painful.

Almost immediately, my magic began healing my wounds. I felt the familiar trickle of heat as bones were set back in place. These weren't light wounds. It would take some time until I fully healed—time which I did not have.

The Behemoth turned its gaze once more towards the kid.

Time to call the cavalry. Which sadly, in my case, was the cat.

Slowly, I reached inside my shirt and touched the ruby pendant I always wore. It served as a link between Amaymon and myself, between master and familiar.

"Amaymon, get over here, now," I growled through clenched teeth. Healing magic was all well and good, but it still hurt like hell.

A patch of air in front of me cracked with static and distorted. Amaymon popped from it, flicking his tail in annoyance.

"So, I guess you found the Behemoth," he quipped.

"Save the kid," I rasped.

Amaymon turned his head in the boy's direction and back. "No."

A flash of pain went through me and I felt the last of the broken ribs mending. "What do you mean, no? That's an order," I growled.

"Erik, I'm your familiar, not your butler. You do something for me and I do something for you. That's how this works." Amaymon's intense yellow eyes bore a challenge.

I stood up and looked around for my gun. It had disappeared during my brief moment as a crash test dummy.

"So, what's in it for me?" he asked. "And I suggest you decide quickly. That thing looks like it's about to pounce at any second."

"Fine. What do you want?" I asked exasperatedly.

The Behemoth's shadow loomed over the boy. I could smell urine in the air.

"Two belly rubs a day for the next week and an extra-large jumbo box of cookies," Amaymon replied.

I looked at him incredulously.

"I'm a cat, Erik. There are only so many ways you can please me."

"Fine, whatever, you got a deal. Now, go!"

The cat had already vanished.

The Behemoth's colossal body concealed the boy and I couldn't see anything. I heard another loud roar and the monster turned abruptly. There was no blood or signs of violence. Amaymon had gotten to the boy just in time.

Sword in hand, I rushed at the beast. A streak of azure energy arced towards one leg. The Behemoth was sent toppling forwards, the ground shaking under the massive weight.

One of its claws swiped at me, but I easily evaded it. My

magic encased Djinn's blade, elongating it. With the demon on the ground, I began hacking and slashing at it, and took advantage of the monster's momentary disadvantage. But all I could do was slash through the black fur—the Behemoth's skin was too thick for even my sword to slice through.

It swung its trunk at me and luckily caught me with just muscle and not the blades. As I rolled away like a rag doll, something hard bumped in my back. Instinctively, my hand went to feel around and the gun I'd lost earlier was back in my possession.

The Behemoth closed the distance and tried a different approach—squash the puny wizard. It raised a paw the size of a garbage can and stomped on me. I raised Djinn and put all my magic there. The Behemoth's paw pressed against the blade.

This was a losing battle—the damn thing was ten times my size.

I shifted my body so I could point my gun at its underbelly. The flintlock roared twice. Thick, black chunks flew off the Behemoth, causing it to rear back in agony.

Fear is as good a motivator as any. Emotion fuels intention, which in turn fuels magic. So, in my near hysterical state, I swung the blade again. A giant crescent-shaped beam of energy shot towards the beast and sent it flying.

I followed its trajectory, batting away trunk and tusks, until I found the beast's mouth. It was similar to an elephant's but with a row of teeth the size of my head. I jammed the gun inside its mouth and squeezed the trigger.

If I couldn't beat it from the outside, then I had to attack it from the inside.

Magic encased the shotgun shell as it tore through its throat and neck, but the Behemoth still trashed around, very much alive.

I channeled more magic into the gun and fired again. There was a small explosion of angry red light as a magically enhanced bullet tore the beast open from the inside. I pulled both my arm and weapon out of its mouth and leapt away.

The Behemoth fell on its side, finally dead.

I slumped on the ground, breathing heavily. I felt my heart pounding in my ears but a burst blood vessel was the least of my worries. There was a moment of hysteria as I sat on my ass watching a hulking monster carcass slowly melt down into opaque ectoplasm. It felt very much like the story of David and Goliath, except I had a gun not a slingshot.

Much more western.

Amaymon appeared at my side. "Mission accomplished?"

"Yeah."

"You got any plans for that ectoplasm?" he asked.

Ectoplasm was to monsters what blood was to humans. A wizard could get very creative with the correct ectoplasm and enough connections. It was a very common ingredient in most textbook spells and rituals. Most shops had the cheap stuff; selling a Behemoth's ectoplasm was like selling a Rolls Royce to a car dealer.

I hadn't really thought about it. I was too busy trying to avoid getting cut or stomped or eaten by a giant mutated elephant. So, all I could offer Amaymon was a shrug.

Cats can't roll their eyes but Amaymon got damn close. "Turn me human and gimme the gun," he said.

"Why?"

"Because that's high-grade stuff right there," he replied. "If I infuse that ectoplasm into your gun, it'll become a channel. A proper magical channel."

"Can you do that?"

I knew it was possible, but the magic had been long lost. The druids had been the last ones to possess that knowledge, but most of their teachings were long gone. My sister might have something in her library, but reading about something and actually knowing how to do it were two very different things.

Amaymon scoffed at me. "Oh, ye of little faith."

I took off my ruby pendant and attached it to his collar. Amaymon may not be the most trustworthy of familiars, but he did know his way around magic. Besides, I didn't have anything to lose.

I felt him call upon his old powers and his form shimmered. In his place was a stocky teenage boy wearing a black tank top, black cargo pants and a black beanie. His eyes were the only feature which remained the same, still cat-like and full of promises of chaos and destruction.

"No funny business," I warned as I handed him the gun.

He smiled, exposing a set of serrated, shark-like teeth. The weapon twirled around his finger as he approached the puddle of disappearing ectoplasm. He stuck a finger in and tasted the gooey stuff.

"Oh, yeah," he said approvingly. When in human form, Amaymon adopted an urban accent. I don't know why, but it annoyed a lot of people.

That might be the answer, right there.

"That hit the spot," he said.

"Just get on with it," I said.

Usually a wizard would require the magical equivalent of a butterfly net to interact with something purely ethereal, but not Amaymon. The demon extended one clawed hand and scooped up the ectoplasm like ice cream. He stuffed it into the gun savagely, like a kid putting sand in a bucket. After a while, he raked in the last handful and stuffed it into his mouth.

"Done," he said, tossing my gun back at me.

It felt lighter, yet at the same time more solid.

"I stuffed all I could in it," continued my familiar. "Couldn't fit all of it, but that gun should be able to take whatever punishment you put it through."

"Cool. Thanks," I said holstering my weapons. "Guess this makes me even with my sister."

Amaymon's eyebrow shot up. "I think she still owes you one, bro."

"Nah. Remember that time," I said scratching my forehead, "with the vampires-"

"Oh, right," he interjected.

"-and the whole camera incident-"

"Dude, they put your ass on MySpace."

"Yeah, and she covered for me," I said. "So, now it makes us even."

Amaymon was about to retort with something, but the wailing of police sirens cut him off.

"Cops," he muttered. "We better hustle."

"That was fast."

Amaymon gave me a sly smile. "I may have left the kid at the nearest police station."

"Sometimes I think your existence is just to torment me."

"It's not my only reason to exist, but it does take up most of my time," he replied. With a flick of his wrist, he ripped at the air and a portal shimmered. "But I guess I'm both the creation and the solution of all your problems."

I made a face at the portal. "I hate those things," I complained. Traveling through portals made me sick to my stomach.

Amaymon smiled even wider. It made him look like the Cheshire Cat. Or the Joker.

"Two minutes 'til we're ass deep in cops," he said.

"How is it you gotta blackmail me to help out a kid and now you're all helpful?" I asked.

Amaymon stepped behind me and tripped me forward. I was sent through the portal with the grace of a tumbling sea lion. We emerged outside of my office and my stomach lurched. Amaymon leaned over as I hurled chunks.

"Because it's highly amusing," he whispered cruelly. His evil laughter echoed throughout the empty street.

Chapter 7

Life tended to be pretty simple for normal folks. You get up, go to work, do something after work that makes you hate life just a little less and then go to bed.

Repeat the following day.

Here's how life worked for me: get interrupted during sleep, deal with clients, confront monsters and psychos, try not to strangle the cat, and go to bed, if at all possible. I had just confronted five lizardmen and a Behemoth. I think I deserved some fucking sleep.

But no, Erik gets no sleep.

This particular nightly interruption was a premonition of sorts. I've been through some weird stuff throughout my career but this was a unique experience.

All of a sudden I was a stranger, like an out of body experience. And just to shake things up a bit, I was a girl. A pretty one, but a girl nonetheless.

First came the flashes. I was a waitress at a coffee shop because I remembered serving clients. I also remembered getting hit on quite a lot, much to my annoyance. Then, I remembered running down an alleyway from something—something dark and evil.

Something that was chasing *me*.

I remembered running away towards my college dormitory and made my way to my room. My roommate was there and I felt she was someone I could trust. I remembered talking to her and she dismissed my worries, blaming it on stress.

But even as she smiled and comically waved her hands, I could still see the worried glint in her eyes.

Another flash and I was at a party. My roommate had dragged me out with her to blow off some steam. I didn't really feel like partying, so I made my way towards the small swimming pool at the very back of the house. I liked the way light reflected off of the water. There was something soothing about it.

A few seconds later, she came into view, a vision of utter beauty.

Her high heels rapped against the floor as she approached me. The shadows slowly peeled off, revealing an epitome of the female human form. Her pale skin glistened under the moonlight as her jet black hair danced sensually over her shoulders and chest. Those wavy curls seemed to end in an even darker shade of black than the atmospheric darkness around. Her blue dress hugged her immaculate body like a second skin and her eyes completed her godly image.

As she came within speaking distance, her eyes sparkled in an amethyst hue. I stared deep into them, completely spellbound. Never in my life did I feel drawn so strongly towards another person. I wanted to both ravage her and worship her—I felt like I could cry just by staring at her. Her eyes seemed to burn a hole in my soul.

Were her pupils always elongated, like a cat's, or was it just a trick of the light?

"Are you all right?" Her voice rang like a note from a pan flute.

"Y-yes, I'm fine," I stuttered. I felt my body temperature rise as she got very close to me. She smiled, revealing dimples that nearly gave me a heart attack.

"Lovely night," she said as she turned those beautiful eyes toward the starry heavens. "It has been too long since I had the time to stop and admire a night such as this."

As she spoke there was a voice screaming in my head, telling me that something was very wrong. It felt a lot like being in the jungle with a tiger. You can't help but stare in awe at the majesty before you, at the raw power that can tear you to shreds. You knew there was absolutely no competition, that this was the tiger's ground, and that you could do nothing save struggle in vain.

That voice in my head let out a second warning, similar to the one I felt when seeing those shadows and sensing danger on my way from work. Except this time it was on a much larger scale.

Despite the warnings, I wanted to lick the very ground she stood on and beg her to make me her slave. If only she spat on me, I would be more fulfilled than I ever had been.

But all I could do was stay there, rooted on the spot and

nodding effervescently.

"I used to enjoy many nights like this with my former lover." Her voice darkened all of a sudden. "That is, until that weak-willed bastard grew fond of another and threw me out into Hell itself."

Anger rose from her like a tidal wave and the area around us seemed to darken.

She leaned forward. "But luckily, I now have many, many children to keep me company," she whispered. Her lips twisted into a pleasant smile that failed to reach her eyes as they turned wild, feral, and full of lust.

"You have kids?" I asked. Her sudden change had upset and confused me but I tried to keep the conversation going—anything to keep her attention on me.

"How nice. How old are they? What are their names?" I asked.

The woman beamed pleasantly. "Oh, I have many children. I know as a parent you're not supposed to have favorites, but we all do, don't we? I like my asmodaii the best. So sweet, so obedient," she cooed.

"What a weird name," I managed to say before fog filled my mind and the world began spinning. I found it hard to focus on anything. My heart rate sped up and I felt the very air around us thicken.

"Do not worry. It will all be over soon," I heard her say. Her voice was melodic, yet it had none of the previous beauty. This was not the song of a siren but the menacing growl of a predator toying with its food.

Pain flared in my shoulder as she laid a slender hand on

it to hold me in place.

She leaned forward, her motion very deliberate. A moist tongue trickled down the length of my neck. I heard faint crackling coming from her mouth as her neat set of pearly white teeth shifted into a row of fangs. With one swift movement she struck, digging into my neck. Blood gushed forth, trickling down my body.

I was helpless to do anything except wait for that creeping darkness to overtake me. The last thing I remembered was the feeling of falling and the rush of cool water against my skin.

I back in my regular body now, but there was still nothing I could do except stare at the red-headed girl floating face up in the pool as blood was mixed in with the water.

Suddenly there was a flash of light, like a supernova going off. But calling it simply a light would have been like calling the sculpture of David a carving or the Mona Lisa a doodle.

It was light with power, a light that was alive. I felt its power radiate into me, giving me strength. Not that it helped. I was a specter, a useless observer intruding on a very disturbing dream.

But the woman, the vampiric monster who just tore a hunk of flesh from the girl's neck, screamed and recoiled.

"This isn't over," she snarled, before disappearing back into the darkness.

And just like that it was over. I watched as the poor girl floated spread-eagle in the pool.

Protect the girl, a disembodied voice echoed inside my head.

There was no question, or request. The voice spoke with such power that I felt myself compelled to obey. The idea of saying no was non-existent to me.

Another flash and we were now in a hospital room. The redhead girl lay there with wires and pipes in her arms as nurses patched up her wound. For the first time, I could see the details of her face. She was very pretty, in an earthly kind of way. None of that superficiality—she was a natural beauty.

Protect her.

There was that voice again, echoing in my head like a madman with a megaphone. This time I was ready for it, and when the voice echoed again I could still retain a portion of my analytical mind and try to figure out who, or what, was talking to me.

It was a message in a bottle. Problem was, these mystical disembodied voices rarely gave you any real investigative information. Like, for example, a name or an address.

Instead they spewed clichés and messages of impending doom.

I could hear her heart monitor in the background.

Beep beep.

Then, a new sound, like the ringing of a bell. That can't be right. No heart monitor rang like a bell on those hospital dramas where everyone sleeps with each other and then they spend entire seasons trying to figure out their feelings.

"Wake up, Erik." It was a familiar voice, maybe Amaymon's.

I ignored it, pining for a few more moments of sleep.

Maybe I would dream about a sandy beach full of models in bikinis this time.

A sudden flash of pain jerked me awake. I felt my arm on fire and looked down to see blood oozing from four deep scratches on my arm.

Looking up, I caught a glimpse of the cat's tail disappearing from my room.

"What was that for?" I yelled as I rubbed my face. The doorbell rang again.

"Answer the freakin' door, dumbass. I'm trying to sleep here."

Chapter 8

Whoever was behind the door rang again. If this was another door-to-door salesperson, there will be a murder today.

Who in their right mind would ring a door bell at nine in the morning?

"Whatever you're selling, I don't give a-" I stopped mid-sentence and looked at the girl standing on my porch. Tanned, possibly Latina, medium height and piercing black eyes. I stared at her as if I'd seen an apparition. This chick was quite literally the girl from my dreams. Well, one of them at least.

She was the redhead's roommate.

"Mr. Ashendale?" she asked.

"Yeah, that's me. Can I help you?"

Her face lit up, suddenly hopeful. "Mr. Ashendale, I've heard that you are able to solve certain problems that others cannot."

I raised my eyebrows, waiting for more details.

There was a screening process to my clientele. When you

dealt in the supernatural, skeptics and religious nut jobs made up most of your clients. Most just wanted to see a performance and, when I left them disappointed, they weaseled out of paying me. Over the past couple of years I've refused twice as many clients as I'd helped out. And just because I dreamt about her, that didn't automatically give her a pass.

"I'm gonna need a little more than that, lady. But if you're looking for a dare or something to blow your mind, I'm sure Criss Angel is still around," I said.

Her eyes flashed in panic. "Mr. Ashendale, please, I'm not trying to fool you." Panic: that was a hard one to fake. The despair in her eyes looked real, too. "Please, hear me out. I will give you a token of faith," she said.

Token of what now?

"This should be good," I muttered.

"You're a wizard, right? Which means that you can do all kinds of mind control stuff just by knowing a person's name, right?" she asked.

"Not as much as you'd think, but sure, yeah, I could."

Truth be told, that was more of an urban legend. I could have harmed her just as easy even without her name. Personal details were only good for bloodline curses or thaumaturgy. That wasn't really my style—I was more direct.

Fireball-to-the-face direct.

"My name is Gracie Valdez." She looked around. Was she expecting to randomly blow up or something?

"My friend Abigail was seriously hurt last night. You're

the only one who can help her," she continued.

My heart sank.

"Is Abigail a redhead by any chance?" I asked, already knowing the answer.

Gracie's eyes widened. "How do you know that?"

"Lucky guess. Come on in."

"So, let me get this straight," I said. I was pacing around my desk while Gracie sipped on some coffee. "Your roommate was at a party, got assaulted, and is now in the hospital. Why not call the police?"

"I did. But there's more." She seemed to struggle to find the right words. "Abigail always had this thing about her. She could sweet talk anyone. She was nice and comforting and always attracted people to her."

"Sounds like one of those charismatic types to me," I said, rolling my eyes.

I didn't like charismatic people. Women always fell for them and I considered that cheating. It should be a level playing field.

I supposed that was just a long, convoluted way of me wishing I was a charming guy.

"Yes, she is," Gracie replied. "Recently she's been very spooked. She felt like she was being watched. A few days ago she came running to our dorm saying something was chasing her."

She looked me in the eye. "I know it's not much, but I'm really scared for her. And now she's in the hospital after some psycho woman bit her neck. She could have died." Gracie shifted uncomfortably and reached inside her purse. "Money is not an issue."

I sighed. I wished this was all just about the money. Even under normal circumstances the case seemed genuine enough. But then there was that dream, a series of visions, like a person's memories.

Abigail's memories.

Somehow, somewhere, a being powerful enough to invade my mind wanted me to take the case. I was tempted to say no there and then, purely out of spite. I hated following orders.

But if I did, the girl would suffer. She would probably be targeted again. Heck, it might be too late already. I could already be investigating a murder instead of an assault.

It was the light that sold me. When I heard that reverberating voice screaming '*protect the girl*' in my head I felt something stir inside me. Something I hadn't felt in a long time.

Or rather, I didn't want to remember the last time.

This case, this girl, was somehow connected to my curse. I didn't know how I knew that—I just did.

But I wasn't about to say yes that readily. People like me tended to live longer if they were just a little too paranoid.

"How come your friend lived?" I asked Gracie.

The girl choked on her coffee. "What do you mean?"

"She ended up in the hospital, right? Hospitals don't take dead people. So, how come she's still kicking?"

Gracie shrugged. "I guess she got lucky."

I raised an eyebrow. "First lesson in this world, there is

no luck." I leaned against the table. "I think you know exactly what happened. And for some weird reason you're not telling me."

"I am telling you all I know, Mr. Ashendale."

"Then explain the white light."

Funny how one simple sentence can cause such a big reaction.

Gracie's eyes widened in something that was either pure shock or horror, or a mixture of both. Either way, I had scored a point there.

"That's the funny thing about dreams," I said. "Some you never remember, but others just keep replaying themselves over and over in your brain like a broken record. And here's the kicker. Once you get over the main events, you start focusing on the little details. Like how you were first on site after Abigail fell bleeding into the pool, even though you were the farthest from her."

I rested both hands on the desk like a cop during an interview scene.

Try not to judge—this was my moment.

"So, you are either on the bad guy's side and were waiting for Abigail to die, or you knew that she had a means of protection."

"No, I-"

"Just give me the whole truth, Gracie," I insisted, cutting her off. "I don't like half-assed stories. Because usually I don't end up getting paid."

Amaymon chose that particular time to show just how much of a wiseass he can be.

"Not to mention the fact that you risk burning half your actual ass."

On reflex I arched my head back and yelled, "That happened one time!"

Then I remembered that cats didn't talk and I had a regular, sane human sitting on my couch.

Gracie sat very still with her eyes wide open, and slowly turned to look at the cat. And despite the latin tinge in her skin, she was white as a sheet.

Oh, crap.

Chapter 9

Gracie's mouth opened but no sounds came out. The cat just stood there, right by the kitchen entrance, as if daring her to say something. Finally enough of her rational mind came back online to make sense of the situation.

"Oh, my God, the cat just talked!"

My first reaction was to reply with something sarcastic, but I decided to cut the girl some slack. Better she state the obvious than run away screaming.

Less likely for the cops to show up at my door later.

"Yes, it talks," I confirmed. "Although sometimes I wish it didn't. Sometimes I wish it could just obey simple instructions like *stay away from clients*. I'd be happy with a cat that just meows."

"It talked!" she yelled again.

This was getting us nowhere.

I leaned in and gently grasped her hands. "Yes, the cat talks."

I laughed, hoping to reassure her. "I'm a wizard with a

talking cat. It's a cliché, I know, but at least I follow the archetype." I squeezed her hands just a little, enough to gain her attention. "I'm gonna need you to accept that and move on. I need to know the full story, about what happened with your friend Abigail."

The girl completely ignored me. I could feel her shaking as Amaymon approached her and leapt into her lap. That cat had absolutely no sense of boundaries. He stared at her for a second and the only sound was his purring.

"Relax, Erik," he said, breaking the silence. "She's not gonna snap."

He turned his head in my direction and let out a meow.

"Can't you tell? She's a practitioner," he said as his tail flicked in annoyance. "And I ain't the weirdest thing she's seen. What are you trying to pull here, lady?"

Actually, I couldn't tell.

Stupid, Erik.

I should have read her aura the moment as she entered the door. Or maybe upgrade my security system to zap anyone or anything magical, rather than use the low energy one I had right now. Sure, it was a pain in the ass to activate and maintain but at least I wouldn't have these kinds of surprises.

Thank God Amaymon was more attentive than I was. Guess the cat had a use after all.

"I don't know what you're talking about," she said, but now that I knew she was lying I could see through her disguise.

It was in the subtle details. The tone of voice, flicks of

hair, the pursing of lips. She must have realized it was a losing battle because she wasn't even bothering to lie anymore.

"Are you a practitioner?" I asked.

"Yes," she replied. "Yes, I am."

"So, that's why you gave me your name," I said.

"We don't like it when people fuck around with us," Amaymon said threateningly.

"No, no, I swear. What I said is all true." She had her hands in the air and all pretense was now gone.

"And Abigail?" I asked. "She a practitioner, too?"

"No, she's not."

"Then what is she?"

Gracie looked from the cat to me and closed her eyes, like she was betraying some sort of secret.

"She's a succubus."

There was a stunned pause.

"A succubus?" I looked at her intently. "Do you even know what that is?"

"I do. And you could use a couple around here, Erik," shot the cat.

Ouch. Kitty, one. Wizard, zero.

Gracie rolled her eyes and gave me an annoyed look. "Of course I know what that is. She's a temptation demon."

Temptation—that was a nice way of saying people drool over her.

Succubii were half-demons, and their main power was seducing people into breeding with them. They're not the most social of monsters, usually popping up when they had an itch to scratch and then would disappear again. Which begs the question: what the hell was a succubus doing at a college dorm?

I mean, I heard stories about college parties, but this was just taking it too far.

"Why is a succubus in your dorm?" I asked with a chuckle. "Are you guys some sort of supernatural sorority or something?"

Gracie gave me look that Clint Eastwood would have been proud of.

"No. There's no sorority," she replied icily. "It's just me who knows about magic. Abigail has no idea what she is. She's only nineteen."

Succubii generally manifest around the age of twenty. That's when their sex drive takes over and they start humping their way through life. Until then, they're pretty much regular folk.

Very pretty, very sexy, regular folk.

"Are you going to tell her?" I asked seriously.

"I don't know," she said, shaking her head. "She's different, you know? I read somewhere that her kind exhibit signs of sociopathy, but she's the sweetest person I know. No way she'll become a monster."

"I'm not in the business of protecting monsters," I replied.

The implication was clear. I would kill the succubus if she became dangerous. I was even considering killing her now when she still hadn't killed anyone, but the virtuous side of me decided to let her commit a crime before executing her.

Innocent until proven guilty and all that.

But the ruthless side of me knew that human justice did not apply to monsters. Once her instincts took over, she would kill. Better to prevent a crime rather than wait for one and give chase.

Gracie's eyes hardened, matching my expression. "She's not a monster. But she is being targeted by one. She's the victim here, Mr. Ashendale, and unless you help her, she will die."

I had no reply to that.

So I decided to deal with one issue at a time. First comes the rescue of a yet-still-innocent girl. Dwelling on moral issues wasn't going to help anyone. I decided to cross that bridge when I was faced with it.

"She's got you there, Erik," said the cat.

"Fine," I said. "But if she makes one move out of line, she's dead. You hear me? She gives me any reason to be wary of her and I'll eliminate her on the spot. No warning, no mercy. Got it?"

Gracie nodded sharply.

"Okay, then." I sat down on the couch facing her. "Tell me about the white light. What was that?"

"An angel."

It took me a whole minute before yelling, "Oh, come on!"

"I'm sorry," she said. My outburst had caused her to jump in her seat. Amaymon just snickered.

"An angel? Are you kidding me?" I rubbed the bridge of

my nose. "Are you sure?"

"It told me it was," she replied.

Huh? It *told* her?

Angels weren't exactly known for their social skills. If they ever made it out of Heaven, their home dimension, then it was only to smite some demon. Their sole purpose was to tip the balance of Earth towards order, as opposed to the demons' chaos.

So, when people came around saying angels talked to them, my first instinct was to check them into a loony house. You've got a better chance of getting probed by aliens from Jupiter than to cross paths with an actual angel, much less have a conversation with one.

"She ain't lyin', Erik," Amaymon said.

"Did you summon it?" I asked.

That tended to happen a lot with practitioners. They see something in a book or grimoire and try it out. Half of the monsters in this world were the result of curious teenagers poking around in the wrong places. Although angels were as heavyweight as you could get. You can't just summon them. They were way too powerful for humans, even for a group of wizards. It just didn't happen.

"No, it just appeared in a dream. It said its name is Jehudiel and it'll be watching over Abigail," Gracie replied with a casual shrug.

Clearly she had no idea of the impact of what she was saying. She may as well have said that she had a summer residence in Shamballa and rode to school on Nessie, the Lock Ness Monster.

I didn't know angels had names. I mean, sure, the Bible is full of them, although most are just symbolic titles, invented by some friar who was eager to impress with his knowledge of Latin, philosophy, and whatever crap the clergy wanted to listen to.

"What's the big deal?" Gracie asked. "If an angel is protecting her, then it's a good thing, right? I mean they are the good guys."

"Not exactly," Amaymon said. He sat on her lap. "Angels have their own agenda: conquer through law and order. Not to mention the fact that they are completely obsessed with their war with Hell. If they are showing up here, then it's only a matter of time."

"Before what?" she said.

"The apocalypse," Amaymon replied in a spooky tone.

"Stop scaring the girl, Amaymon," I said.

"But it's so easy."

"Give it a rest," I said before turning back to Gracie. "Forget everything he's told you. It's probably a mistake of sorts."

"They don't make mistakes like that," the cat interjected.

"Shut up," I shot back. It seemed to work.

Joking usually made the regular ones question how deep the grave they dug was. It worked even better when you left out the end of the world theories.

Gracie looked at me, then down at cat. She was going to have one heck of a story to tell. She might even write us in a television pilot: the Wizard and Kitty Show.

"I'll take the case," I said. "But do yourself a favor and

disappear. Find somewhere remote and lather it in as many charms and protective spells as you can."

"Why?"

"'Cause you're in deep now." I looked at her intently, the humor completely gone from my voice. "You're caught in the middle of a celestial war which humanity has avoided for years. And in every war there is collateral damage, namely people like you. So, run and hide and don't come out until I say so."

She nodded and rose to leave.

"Thank you, Mr. Ashendale."

I waved her off. "Call me Erik. And leave that cheque on the table."

"The money ain't worth it."

I waved the cheque at the cat. "You say that now, but wait 'til we're out of food. Besides, I'm kinda curious to see where all this goes."

"So, what now then?" he asked. "Wait and see what pops out and then shoot it in the face?"

"You got it," I said as I picked up the phone.

"Dialing heaven?" Amaymon asked as he hopped on the desk beside the phone.

"More like Hell on Earth."

There was a tone dial and Mephisto's cold voice crackled on the other end of the line. "Good morning, Ashendale mansion. How may I help you?"

"'Sup, doggie," I said enthusiastically. "Where's Gil?"

"Master Gil is busy," he replied. "May I take a message?"

"Yeah, tell her I have an angel running around and that it might be in her best interest to stop ignoring me and PICK UP THE PHONE!"

That should get her attention. Sure enough, there was a shuffle at the other end as the receiver exchanged hands.

"What do you want, Erik?"

Gil was not a happy girl.

"Hi, Gil." The glee in my voice probably didn't help her mood.

"What. Do. You. Want?" she growled in a voice that promised my imminent death. As I said, Gil does not like to lose.

"I got a new case," I said in a chipper tone.

"Good for you."

"It involves an angel."

"How so?"

"It seems to be protecting someone," I said. Better not include that detail about the succubus. "Ever heard of a Jehudiel?"

I heard the tapping of a keyboard at the other end. "Seems to be an archangel," she said. Then a few seconds later, "Huh."

"What?" I asked.

"Says here he's a Virtue. Never heard of that."

"Why not ask your bodyguards?" I said, remembering the entourage she had with her.

"They don't do interviews, Erik." A sigh crackled on the other end of the phone. "Erik, is this so-called person in reality a succubus?"

Oh, crap.

"Maybe."

"Oh, God, Erik."

"What?"

"My angels are after the succubus," she said.

"So, what about this Jehudiel guy?"

A groan escaped her throat. "I don't know. Maybe we're dealing with a rogue here."

"A rogue angel?" I asked as I looked at Amaymon. He just cocked his head to one side and remained quiet.

"Either way, I'm gonna need you to step down from this one," she said.

"Step down?" I did not like where this was going.

"Yes," she replied. Her voice suddenly hardened. "A word of warning: we're going after this succubus. Do not stand in my way."

"Or what?" I challenged.

"Or I'll crush you, too."

All that was missing was the theme from *The Good, the Bad and The Ugly* playing in the background.

"Why are you doing this, Gil?"

"Because I have to," she spat. "Because this goes all the way to the top. There are things in play here that far outweigh whatever case you have. So, listen well: Drop. The. Case."

She shouldn't have said that. I don't follow orders, ever. It's like telling a kid not to do something. They end up doing exactly what you tell them not to.

If this went all the way to the top, then it was no longer

in Gil's hands. And as much as she irritates me, I'd much rather she be the top dog around here. Whoever she was answering to might not have the Earth's best interest in mind.

And that did not sit well with me at all.

If the angels were in charge, then all was lost already. But I had the feeling she was getting pressure from a third party, someone deep in the shadows but powerful enough to force the Ashendale leader into action.

Someone like a super secret organization of wizards with whom Gil had ties with. These guys were so paranoid that even uttering their name could get you in serious trouble.

Either way, I wasn't about to drop the case. If anything, I wanted to see this until the end.

"No way, sis," I challenged. "I'm seeing this through."

"Funny you should say that. Good luck then, brother."

She hung up the phone just as Amaymon waded in. "So what's our next - Erik, duck!"

But his warning registered too late.

A series of explosions went through my office. Shrapnel flew in every corner as bullets ripped into my arm and side. I threw myself painfully on the ground and my lungs felt as if they were on fire.

I felt my healing powers take effect. Projectiles were ejected from my arm. They weren't the usual deformed bullets, but thin shards of iron shrapnel.

I heard the sound of boots crunching glass.

A guy walked in, wearing heavy combat boots and black cargo pants. His biker jacket revealed a bodybuilder's torso.

I inched beyond the table's edge. His weapon was not a firearm but a long barrel extending from where his forearm should be.

In his other hand he held a cell phone to his ear.

"Yeah, boss. I got him. Call you when I'm done here."

He pocketed his phone. I heard the creaking of metal and watched as his other arm melted and became a long barrel of dark grey iron, matching the one he already had. He sucked in a deep breath and lifted both barrels.

"Say hello to my little friend!" he hollered in a very bad Pacino impression.

Shrapnel flew everywhere as the barrels roared like machine-guns.

"Do you feel lucky, punk?"

Seriously, how many movies was this guy going to ruin for me today?

The barrage stopped abruptly and I peaked from behind my cover, just in time to see him slumped over, clearly exhausted.

Most of my injuries had healed by now and pain was replaced by seething anger. I crouched behind the desk and grabbed the edges. Magic coursed through my body, giving me a burst of strength. The heavy desk was sent flying into the thug, knocking him backwards.

I ran and jumped over the table, practically landing on the guy. My arm met his neck and drove him to the ground. He landed so hard, he actually cracked the floorboards.

I leveled my gun at his face.

"Didn't you get the memo, kid? I'm the only wiseass around here."

Chapter 10

The gun roared in my hand and a loud, metallic sound echoed around the office.

I peered over to see his head completely covered in steel, as if he were some sort of robot. The bullet ricocheted off, leaving only a shallow grove on his forehead.

"What the hell?"

A metal-covered fist connected with my hip. I buckled and fell hard.

We both lay there, moaning in pain.

"Is that whole no-shirt thing some sorta fashion statement?" I said between clenched teeth.

"What's wrong with what I wear?"

"You look like a cross between a biker and that werewolf kid from *Twilight*," I said.

"Like you're any better."

As he said that I saw his arm liquefying and morphing into a long, sharp blade of dark metal. With a grunt he swung his weapon at me. I rolled and managed to avoid being beheaded, but still felt a small cut on my neck. I brought the gun around at the same time that he swung his weapon around, ripping the firearm from my grip.

A second blade—his other arm—stabbed at me.

I sidestepped and felt the blade tear through my shirt. I quickly glanced down but saw no permanent damage. Pissed off, I charged at him and lunged.

My elbow met his nose and I felt something crunching. Still keeping my momentum, I spun, kicked backwards and sent him flying over my shoulder in classic judo throw.

He landed heavily on his back and I smirked.

I saw his arms shift shape again, reverting back into guns. These had shorter barrels than the ones he used when he made his entrance. He grunted with effort, lifting his weapons to hip level and gunfire erupted from them. I leapt backwards and crossed my arms.

Normally I can't use magic without any channels, but I found a loophole to that: a set of crystals placed inside the walls of my office which allowed me to manipulate magic freely inside my own home.

I crossed my arms and an invisible shield of energy formed in front of me. It robbed the bullets of their kinetic energy, causing them to fall harmlessly on the ground.

The guy got to his knees and his weapons disappeared.

"You're tougher than I imagined," he rasped between heavy pants.

"You're no pushover either," I replied. "For a young elemental anyway."

"How did you know?" he asked with a growl.

I could have gone into a Sherlock Holmes-esque explanation. I could have told him that novice elementals had trouble producing their respective element, so they use what's already there. In this case, the iron from his own blood. All he had to do was multiply it over and over again.

But what I did say was, "I'm an almighty wizard."

I laughed at his frustrated look.

"And I also know you're just about ready to collapse," I continued. His expression confirmed just how spot on I was and I just grinned.

"Quit while you still can, kid, or else you're in for a world of hurt," I added.

"Yeah, right."

I held up two fingers. "I'll knock you out in two strikes. Then, you'll be so impressed with my awesomeness that you'll answer my questions."

He got to his feet. Metal crept over his body like ink blotting on a piece of paper, slowly encasing his body in dark iron.

"Screw you," he said in a voice that seemed to echo. It must be the metal around his mouth and throat that gave him his cool robot voice.

I opened my arms in challenge. "Have it your way, kid."

He charged at me with a feral snarl.

I shifted sideways and extended my magic over the area around me. The air became heavy and damp as moisture gathered. A torrent of water crashed into the elemental from all directions, swirling around him in a violent current. He hung suspended in a water prison, gasping for air.

Soon, the first patches of rust appeared sporadically. The dark spots grew, hindering his powers and movement even more.

I held up my index finger. "One down."

Static crackled around me and arced down to my fingertips. Tiny bolts of electricity zapped angrily from my hands. I was grinning so wide, it was hurting my cheeks.

"Join the Dark Side of the Force," I yelled maniacally.

I had to admit it, I looked damn cool. Just like a Sith Lord.

Darth Erik.

I sent the lightning towards the elemental.

The water amplified the electricity and the resulting explosion literally rocked the ground. The elemental's metal body acted as a lightning rod, taking in a million of volts of damage.

There was another, louder explosion and a bright flash of light. The water evaporated and I heard the guy scream. The elemental fell on the ground, twitching erratically. He tried to say something but couldn't get his lungs to work. He shuddered some more and fell to the ground, unconscious. His metallic armor flaked off, revealing the regular shirtless guy beneath. Smoke billowed from his body.

That kid was down for good.

Amaymon's little feline head popped from beneath a destroyed wardrobe. "Is it over yet?"

Chapter 11

"Yo, kid. Snap out of it."

I threw a second bucket of cold water at him and slapped him in the face.

He jerked up, suddenly wide away.

I had tied him up to a chair and sat in front of him. There was a circle of chalk drawn around his chair to interrupt the flow of magic. I had also drawn a triangular symbol on his forehead with a sharpie. That was to keep him from focusing on anything for too long.

Like, say, morphing his arm into a sword and slicing my head off. After all there's only so much my healing powers can do.

The guy shook his head. He looked up, recognized me and shot me a dirty look.

"Told you I'd take you down," I said gleefully.

He struggled against his bonds.

"That's not gonna happen," I jabbed.

Clearly I hit him too hard, because he didn't seem to hear

me. Instead, he kept struggling until his face turned red.

"Dance monkey, dance," Amaymon muttered.

I raised my hand and flicked my index finger towards him. A bolt of psychic energy hit the triangle on his forehead. The guy yelled in pain and his head reeled backwards.

"You done?" I asked.

The elemental just panted heavily and glared. He was going to wake up with one giant headache in the morning.

"So," I said. "What's your name?"

"Go blow yourself."

I flicked my finger again, sending a second psychic bolt in his direction. He expressed his pain by letting out a very long stream of curses.

"I'm almost certain that's not your name," I said.

"Shut the-"

"Ah, ah," I warned as I waved my finger threateningly in his face.

He dropped his head in surrender.

"Jack," he finally replied.

I blinked at him, waiting for an elaboration. "Jack. Just Jack," I said raising my eyebrows. "Jack the Elemental."

His frown deepened.

"Okay, Jack," I said. "Who sent you here?"

"I don't know," he spat.

I raised my eyebrow and repeated the spell for a third time. He actually yelped this time.

"Wanna try that again?"

"Son of a-" he began.

I gave him the finger again—not that finger. The painful finger.

You know what I mean.

Jack's voice rose by a couple octaves.

"What's wrong, Jackie-boy? Can't handle a little pain?" I said before turning to Amaymon. "You believe this joker is supposed to be a tough guy?"

"Lemme take over." The cat calmly padded over and hopped on Jack's lap.

"Okay, here's how it's gonna work, Jack," I said. "I ask a question, you lie, the cat messes you up and *then* you tell me the truth."

"Another talking animal?" said the elemental. "I'm not scared of a cat."

Amaymon let out a cute meow that would have made any girl swoon. Then he dug his claws into Jack's thigh and the guy screamed.

"Hey, jackass," the demon said. "You don't talk unless he asks a question."

Intimidation by cat—it never fails.

"Why did you trash my office?" I asked.

Jack eyed the cat warily. "I was paid to beat up some wizard named Ashendale. They said he lived here alone and I'd have the advantage," he blurted out rapidly.

The cat did not torture him again so I assumed he was telling the truth.

"Who are *they*?" I asked.

"They said they'll kill me if I tell," Jack whimpered.

Amaymon scraped his claws into the elemental's trousers.

"If you don't tell us, *I* will kill you," threatened the cat.

"Wait," I ordered. "We can go about this another way."

Good cop, bad cop. Or, in our case, good wizard, homicidal kitty.

"This is bugging me," I said, slowly pacing around. "When you heard Amaymon talk you said, and I quote: 'not another talking animal'. Which means you already met another talking animal, right?"

Jack nodded. "Black dog. Huge damn thing."

I groaned internally. Unless there was another giant talking black dog around, then I was sending my office repair bill to Mephisto. Or Gil.

"Lemme guess," I groaned. "Your boss is a petite blonde with a long braid and a weird costume? Drives around in a limo?"

Jack nodded.

"Ah, crap."

"You know her?" he asked.

"Yes."

"Enemy?"

"Worse," I shot back. "Sister."

Jack laughed. "Good one."

I didn't laugh.

"You're serious?" he asked incredulously.

I rolled my eyes. "What about you, Jack? How come you're a hit man?" I asked, throwing the spotlight back on him.

"I'm not a hit man."

"Good because you're horrible at it," I said. "So, what are

you? Thug for hire?"

Jack lowered his head. "You don't know what it's like to live on the streets. And it's not like you're any better," he replied. "Running some sorta scam out of a fancy office."

I grabbed him by the collar and wedged my face mere inches from his.

"Screw you. I *help* others," I yelled, my voice suddenly quivering with anger. "I use my powers to bring a little peace to this world by getting rid of monsters and idiots like you. I never, *ever,* took money to hurt anyone, even when I lived on the streets at an age younger than yours. So, take your sad story and shove it up your ass."

"Didn't you *escape* the mansion?" Amaymon interjected. Somehow he managed to pull off a mocking expression on his feline face.

"Not now, Amaymon. I'm trying to prove a point here," I shot back.

But I thanked him inwardly. Amaymon knew that getting too emotional about this was not going to solve anything.

"Just getting my facts straight," the cat replied innocently, before resuming the task of scratching the leather fabric of Jack's pants.

I took a deep breath.

Get your head in the game, Erik.

"Did she say where she was going?" I asked turning back to Jack.

The elemental glared. "I heard her mention a hospital," he said.

"Which makes this jackass a distraction," Amaymon said.

I stood up, pushing my chair away. Amaymon was right. What better way to slow me down other than a literal human tank? This type of underhand tactic was just like my sister.

"Let's go," I told Amaymon.

I definitely needed him on this case, especially if Gil was going to go after the succubus with angels and Mephisto in tow.

I scooped up my gear and put on my coat.

"What's in it for me?" Amaymon asked as he hopped off Jack.

I raised my arms in exasperation. "What do you want from me?"

Amaymon's whiskers flicked. "I already told you that. I'm not your pet or your servant. So, what's in it for me?"

"I dunno. Honor?" I suggested. Amaymon stared at me as if I had suggested shaving him.

I tried again, this time in a more upbeat tone, like a game show host.

"How about an adventure, TV remote control for the next week, and a chance to flirt with a succubus? I hear girls find cats adorable."

The cat flicked his tail enthusiastically.

"Sold," he said. "What are we still doing here?"

"Hey, what about me?" called the elemental.

I considered leaving him bound like that, but I don't have the guts for torture. So, I walked towards him, licked my thumb and rubbed my moist finger against his forehead, wiping away the triangle.

"Get out of the rest on your own," I said. "I don't care where you go or what you do. Just don't be here when I get back. If I ever hear of you again, I'll hunt you down myself and terminate you. You understand?"

His eyes widened and he nodded.

There was a motorbike standing outside my office. I guessed it was Jack's.

I'm not much of a bike enthusiast, but even I could appreciate the marvelous piece of engineering in front of me. Either way, I needed a ride, and Jack wasn't going anywhere for a couple of hours. And I figured he owed me for destroying my office.

I climbed on it without a second thought, and turned the key. It was still stuck in the ignition. Amaymon hopped in the space between my legs and dug his claws into the leather of the seat.

"Hmm. We could sell the bike after you get your car from the shop," he suggested, arching his head and gazing at me with one eye. "Did you really end up homeless or were you just trying to burst his bubble?" he asked.

"I did," I replied. "I bailed out of the mansion after the incident with my father. I had no money and no place to go. Until I met Tenzin."

"Ah, yeah. Tenzin," Amaymon said. "That exorcist guy who taught you all about being a goody two-shoes. You gotta tell me the whole story someday."

"Another time," I replied.

That wasn't a story I'd ever told anyone. I guess I didn't

want to acknowledge the fact that he had died to save my life. If I told the story out loud, it would become real, and I didn't want his death to be real. Even after all these years, I knew I still wasn't ready for that.

I shook my head.

Enough dwelling on the past, Erik. You have a sister to beat and a sex demon to rescue.

Chapter 12

"Any luck tracking Gil?" I asked as I swerved around a corner and weaved through a line of slow cars.

"No," the cat replied. "No trace whatsoever. They must be cloaking themselves."

The grayish-white hospital building loomed in sight. Why can't hospitals have upbeat colors? At least it wouldn't be that depressing.

I drove into the underground parking and ditched the bike in a corner.

"Erik, check out that limo," Amaymon called from behind me.

A sleek black vehicle was parked at the opposite end, occupying more than two spaces.

"Gil," we said together.

We bolted to the reception area and I forced my way through to the desk, in between the other patients filling out forms and the small stream of nurses and doctors whizzing by.

"Excuse me," I said to the plump African-American nurse behind the reception desk. She took one look at me and her frown turned suspicious. Before she could ask me to either leave or fill out a form I went straight to the point.

"I'm here to see someone named Abigail. Red hair, short, a college student. Got attacked in the neck. I'm a friend of hers."

"I'm sorry, sir," she curtly replied. "Only family allowed in."

"But I really need to see her," I said in an urgent tone as I scanned the place for any signs of my sister or her posse.

"Sir, I just told you, you're not allowed," she said sternly. "And this is a hospital. You can't bring any animals in here."

I shuffled impatiently. "Look, lady, I get it. You have a job to do. But I have to see this girl. It's a matter of life and death."

Error number one, never ever use the term 'life and death' in a hospital. It doesn't sit well with the hospital staff.

And makes you sound like a terrorist.

"Sir, are you threatening a patient? Or me?"

See what I mean?

"No, not at all. What I meant was-"

"Sir," she interrupted. "You need to leave right now before I call security." She picked up a phone and waved her finger threateningly over the number pad.

Amaymon rubbed against my leg. "Plan B?"

"Plan B," I agreed, not bothering to lower my voice.

Amaymon hopped onto the table and let out a quick hiss. The nurse's eyes rolled into the back of her head and she slumped back in her chair, unconscious. Amaymon padded over a thick ledger and his eyes glowed for a second.

"Room 414," he said.

We raced towards the wards. The cat counted the numbers as we passed them.

"Up ahead, Erik. I feel something," he said as we turned round a corner.

"I feel it, too," I replied.

We saw each other at the same time and froze. Mephisto disappeared inside a ward while Gil lingered back and we engaged in a stunned staring contest.

I charged into a full sprint towards her but it was too late. Gil crossed her arms and spread them forwards. Amaymon shouted a warning but there was little I could do to stop my momentum.

Her spell took effect, creating a giant barrier that reached from the top of the ceiling all the way to the floor, blocking the entire corridor. I crashed into it and pathetically slid down, like an idiotic cartoon character.

Mephisto reemerged with a petite girl hoisted over his shoulder and I caught a glimpse of red hair as both he and Gil turned and went on their way.

"Dammit!" I yelled as I pounded my fist against the invisible wall.

"We can't double back, Erik," Amaymon said. "My brother set up a whole bunch of traps behind us. As soon as we double back, ka-boom!"

"So, we can't go back without blowing up the entire hospital and we can't go forwards cause of my sister's spell,"

I said as my heart started racing with panic.

"Too bad you can't go *over* the building," the cat said.

That's it, I thought. So simple—just go over the building.

"Amaymon, you're a genius," I said as a plan began forming inside my head.

"I know," he replied. Then he frowned. "Wait, why? Are you about to pull something both crazy and dangerous?"

I nodded fervently as I went through my plan again in my head, calculating the possibilities and probabilities. I needed a distraction and the element of surprise.

And with Amaymon I had both.

"Run after their limo and create a diversion. Anything goes. Just don't kill any civilians," I ordered my familiar, fastening the ruby around his collar.

"No holds barred?" he asked. His form simmered and a second later the cat was replaced with a stocky guy, who cracked his neck in anticipation. "You sure about that?"

I nodded. "Just don't hurt anyone. Or wreck the entire city."

"What about your sister?"

"Anything goes," I said darkly.

He flashed his sadistic grin and took off. Once inside a ward he touched the wall and the stone crumbled into dust. He turned, gave me a salute and jumped down, nearly three floors.

At the same time, I walked into the opposite ward and opened the window.

It's not technically correct to say I can't use any magic. My power was too great and too out of control, and as a result it damaged my body. But that only applied to magic outside my body.

But when it comes to using magic inside my body, it was a whole other story. My healing magic was proof of that. It was automatic and could heal just about anything.

And, as long as it was minimal, I could also use other magic, and only if the area of effect was within my own body.

I hopped on the window ledge and magically shifted my center of gravity towards the wall. My body slammed against the wall as if it were a giant fridge magnet. It took a moment for me to get my bearings, but I managed to stand upright—against the side of the hospital building.

One heavy step at a time, I began walking up the wall, like some cheap vampire movie effect.

Yeah, it looked cool.

Until I made the mistake of looking downwards—I mean, backwards—and saw the three-floor drop. Cars skittered about the size of match boxes and all I could think about was how big a stain I would leave if I fell.

As I said, fear was a good motivator.

I steeled myself and fast-walked up that wall like Spiderman on steroids. Finally, I saw the ledge and crouched down. I wrapped my arms and legs awkwardly around the railing and released my spell. My weight fell completely on my hold. I sucked in a deep breath and hoisted myself up. Pain radiated from my legs and I was left paralyzed in agony until the effects subsided.

I said I could use magic but there was always a price to

pay thanks to my curse.

I felt the ground shake and heard people screaming, followed by the screeching of tires.

Yep, that was Amaymon alright. You can always count on him to create chaos.

I ran to the opposite ledge and I saw my sister's black limo skittering around the hospital.

I cursed.

It was supposed to pass a few minutes later, giving me enough time to descend through the fire escape and pincer it from the other side. As it was now, unless I appeared in front of the car in the next ten seconds they would escape, taking the succubus with them.

A swear word slipped through my teeth.

Thank you, Universe, for once again screwing up my awesome plan.

I stood up there, mentally counting down until the car passed directly beneath me and calculated the trajectory of my fall. My brain kept playing images of me squashed into a hamburger.

But despite any reasoning, I still took the leap.

Magically charging up my run, I soared into the air and let out the girliest scream to ever leave my throat.

After the initial ecstasy I felt sharp focus, unlike anything I'd ever felt before. I reached backwards and unsheathed Djinn, holding it in reverse grip. Magic ran through it. There was an explosion of azure light as the energy layer on top of the blade engorged to twice my height. I held the gargantuan sword point down and saw the car getting closer.

And closer.

And then…

BOOM.

Djinn impaled the hood of the car. The limo's body crunched as the front was flattened like a can and the rear end rose upwards and settled back down with a loud crash.

Meanwhile, I was still dangling over Djinn's handle like some sort of charm. My magic faded, returning the short sword back to its original petite size. I slumped down and felt something pop. Both my shoulders had been dislocated. My magic had already begun healing my wounds but I still felt the pain. All I could do was roll on the ground as an "ouch" escaped my lips in a low, pathetic moan.

The limo's door was blasted open and Gil emerged. She sent a ripple of air at me but I managed to roll and avoid most of the damage.

She repeated her spell, knowing full well I couldn't move. A boulder shot up in front of me, shielding me from my sister's magic. Amaymon's figure was spat out from the ground followed by a series of stone spikes that pierced through the undamaged part of the car.

"Control your pet, brother," Gil yelled. "He's going to kill the girl."

"I'm sure your dog is protecting her," I yelled back.

"Erik, get the girl," Amaymon said with glee. He focused on my sister, driving her away with his vicious onslaught.

I had regained the use of my arms by then and extracted my gun. Inside the limo was Abigail, semi-conscious. I reached inside to grab her and a pair of canine jaws clenched around my hand. Mephisto in his dog form, bit down heavily on bone and tendon. His malevolent demonic eyes shone in the darkness and he shook his head, trying to rip off my arm.

I snapped the gun at his face and pulled the trigger. Chunks of flesh tore off but he was otherwise unharmed. His bite got even more vicious and I thought the pain was about to make me pass out.

I dropped the gun and reached inside the leaking gas tank, splashing some of the liquid on his face.

Then I used the same trick I used to burn Roland's cigarette, igniting a spark between my fingertips. The dog's head lit up in a blaze and he let go of my hand. Some gas had gotten on my wrist and I felt the intense burning in addition to the bite injuries. My magic healed my hand as I wrapped it in my coat and choked the flame.

Mephisto appeared in human form above the car, hovering in a gust of wind. Amaymon's element was earth; Mephisto's, the air and wind.

Unlike Amaymon, who beat his opponents down with raw strength, Mephisto was more subtle. He served as the advisor to the Demon Emperor around the same time that Amaymon was leading the army. He knew every trick in the book and he was eager to use them.

And while he was not a frontline fighter like my familiar, he could still do some serious damage. The guy was one of the most ancient demons after all, in addition to being an air elemental. There was no way I could take him down in a straight fight, so I had to cheat.

I waited until the tornado around him had reached its peak and pointed my gun at him.

Time to see if the new toy could withstand some magic.

There was a small red streak as the bullet hit the tornado and burst into flames. The demon instinctively shielded himself and stepped backwards.

Rule number one of surviving a fight with someone tougher than you: never just retreat.

Surprise them, and *then* retreat.

I dove straight for the girl, grabbed her arm and hoisted her over. "Come with me if you want to live."

I know, cheesy. But what do you say to someone in that situation?

I dragged the girl out of the car wreckage just as Mephisto roared in sheer rage.

"Just where do you think you're going with our quarry?" Mephisto asked with a feral look. His teeth were bared, promising slow, deliberate pain.

Out of nowhere, a thick slab of stone crashed right into his face, sending him flying.

Amaymon hollered from across the street. "Hah! In your face, you butt sniffin' creep."

"Mephisto! They mustn't get away," Gil screamed as she crossed her arms and energy gathered around her.

I recognized the spell. She was going to create another barrier, like the one in the hospital. I holstered the gun and grabbed a tire rim. Magic enhanced my throw as I launched the improvised projectile like a discus. It caught Gil in the stomach and she doubled over.

At the same time, Amaymon dug his fingers into the concrete and heaved. The entire street rose and fell back, like a massive carpet roll. Mephisto ran to Gil's side and both of them used wind to counter the earth magic. The result was an explosion and a lot of gavel being thrown about. Amaymon splayed his fingers and debris billowed around them, creating a smokescreen.

"Yo, man, we gotta run," Amaymon said as he pulled both me and the girl around a corner and down the block.

"They can still track us," I said. Mephisto's dog nose wasn't just for show. "Amaymon, I need some clones."

He nodded. From the ground, eight pillars of mud sprouted up. Once grown to about my size, he nodded at me, and I tapped each one, giving them a fraction of my magic. Slowly, their features changed and soon I was staring at eight terra-cotta replicas of myself.

"Do I look that ugly?" I asked Amaymon. "Or is it because they're gray?"

"Nah, it's you," he replied with a grin.

"They smell like you do, and have a trace of your magic in them," he then said, suddenly turning serious. "They will throw off any trackers."

"Okay. I'll take these and make a run for it to distract my sister and Mephisto. You and the girl take another route and meet me at that parking lot in ten minutes," I instructed.

Amaymon nodded and hefted Abigail over his shoulder. The girl offered no resistance. She was either too shocked to move or still groggy from whatever drugs they gave her.

Either way, it was probably for the best that she was out of it.

I took off, going down random streets and alleyways, and deploying the golems in different directions. That was probably enough but I decided to be extra cautious and run around a couple of blocks just in case.

After a few minutes I circled back to the parking lot. A red sedan pulled up next to me and Amaymon grinned from behind the driver's wheel.

"Come with me if you wanna live," he said with a mocking grin.

Chapter 13

Imagine the most awkward drive you've ever experienced. Multiply that by a hundred and add the fear of being followed not only by a mad twin sister, her army of highly trained wizard soldiers, an entourage of angels and Mephistopheles himself, but also a demon that riled up the forces of Heaven with a penchant for redhead succubii.

Now you understand my anxiety.

Abigail, who sat quietly and wide awake in the back seat, only spoke when the car stopped.

"Are you going to kill me?"

I saw the deadpan fear in her eyes and shook my head. Yeah, I could see how it looked—two guys taking a girl from the hospital in a stolen car. Not exactly the swashbuckling rescue I imagined.

"No," I answered. "No one is going to kill you."

"What do you want with me?" she whimpered.

"Believe it or not, I'm here to rescue you."

Her eyes widened and she gazed at my office, with its

bullet-riddled door, shattered glass, and the destroyed furniture. There was a lone chair standing in the middle of all the chaos, where Jack had been tied. The kid was nowhere to be seen.

"We're not kidnapping you either," I reassured her.

Her look told me she wasn't buying it.

"I don't have any money. I'm not even related to anyone important," she said.

Then she smiled gently and came closer.

"Please," she whispered. "Let me go."

I felt her power hit me like a wave. She clearly had no idea how to control herself but she did have some serious juice. I felt pressure in the deepest parts of my brain, the part that pushed me towards very impulsive sexual acts.

That little voice in my head had now been given a megaphone and I wanted nothing more than to obey her and hope for a reward between her legs.

At the same time, I felt another wave of power, this one more familiar.

It was him, Dark Erik. At least, that's how I referred to him. People don't usually have cute pet names for their subconscious but I guess when yours is as active as mine, it's time for a name tag.

Dark Erik was the personification of my curse, of all that power stored inside of me. Power which, for some unknown reason, I just couldn't seem to access.

Unless I was being stabbed, shot or otherwise mutilated.

I could only interact with that power when I meditated deeply enough, and even then, Dark Erik was usually antisocial, much like the real Erik.

Most of the time my subconscious was silent, like a shadow on a wall.

But the moment Abigail's influence pushed against mine, Dark Erik reached inside my head and I felt power taking over me. In an instant her influence was washed away and I felt light as a breeze.

Abigail was still there, aiming those doe eyes at me, probably expecting me to just give in. But when nothing happened she frowned and backed away.

"Nice trick." I cleared my throat. Now, my voice didn't sound so husky. "Not gonna work on me."

"And I suggest you drop that shit unless you really have to," Amaymon said. He leaned back until his face was uncomfortably close to hers.

She recoiled away from him as much as the seat would allow.

Amaymon's feline eyes, especially in his human form, weren't easy to look at. That, and the fact that the guy sorely needed a mint.

"Whoever is chasin' you has already got your scent. My brother has quite the nose on him. So, try not to signal where you are unless you wanna be eaten," he said before wiggling his eyebrows at her. "And not in the fun way."

Did I mention Amaymon is a Class-A pervert? He is. And somehow he managed to get away with it.

Abigail's eyes darted towards me, pleading for my help.

"Back off, Amaymon," I said as I grabbed the collar of his shirt and pulled him back. "You're not helping at all."

"Course I am," he replied.

"Hey," he directed at Abigail. "You gonna use your powers again?"

She shook her head fervently.

He turned to me. "See? Helping."

I rolled my eyes. "Please, ignore him," I gently told the girl. "He's creepy but harmless. How about we go inside? I'm sure the kettle still works. How about some coffee? Tea?"

She remained silent.

It's official: I am the worst negotiator in the world. Ironic since that's exactly what it says on most of my pay slips from the cops.

"I was hired by your friend Gracie," I said, hoping to engage her on some familiar ground. She narrowed her eyes. "She came to see me right after you were admitted into the hospital. I know everything."

"What the hell is going on?" she blurted out.

There it was: the question that confirmed the person's sanity.

There was a very simple way of knowing if a person was normal or not. Put them through a series of inexplicable events, most of which were of a supernatural nature, and just watch their response. If they smiled and accepted it, they were cracked.

Swearing, screaming, and abject panic—those were the good signs.

We made it out of the car and I helped her out. I figured the least I could do after what she'd been through was offer her a hand and a cup of coffee. Amaymon wasn't so helpful. He stumbled on something, cursed, and transformed into a cat.

I felt Abigail's hand tense up.

"Ignore him," I repeated. "He's just trying to impress you. We don't usually have guests. Now you can guess why."

"What happened here?" she asked.

"My sister threw a monkey wrench at me to get to you first," I replied and watched her frown.

"My sister is the blonde midget with the green suit," I clarified.

"What are you people?" she asked for the second time.

I sat her down on the chair and told Amaymon to make us some coffee. Then, I pulled the couch back in place and winced. The whole thing was ruined.

"I'm a wizard," I said plainly. "Name's Erik. Erik Ashendale."

"Did you just say *wizard*?"

"Yes."

"Like Houdini?"

I smiled and glanced at the walls. I sensed that two of the crystals were damaged but I could still use magic freely in the office. So, in a reckless attempt to impress a pretty girl, I conjured up a small fireball in my palm.

"More like Harry Potter," I said as she gasped.

I put the fire out with a *poof*.

"My sister is a type of wizard too," I went on. "She's a Warlock and they're a creepy bunch."

"Are you one, too?"

"Nah. I'm more of a general people-helping wizard," I said.

Amaymon appeared in his human form with our coffee.

"And him?" she asked as she eyed Amaymon. She waited until I took a sip of coffee before sipping hers.

Smart girl.

"Amaymon is a demon," I said.

He raised his eyebrows and beamed at her.

"Why can he transform into a cat?" she asked.

"Because he's my familiar. Speaking of which." I turned towards him and held out my hand. "Give it up."

He hissed and took off the pendant. "Dickhead."

A cat took his place and he settled next to me. "Start patting," he said. "I don't work for free."

He purred loudly as I rubbed his tummy.

"This is so weird,"Abigail said.

"Welcome to my world," I replied. "But this *is* reality, and the sooner you accept it, the better."

She sipped her coffee.

There was a moment of silence until she asked, "So, what am I?"

Whatever I said next could send her over the edge. How do you tell someone they were part demon, that their power was meant to seduce people out of their life force?

Maybe I could ease her into it.

"What can you do?" I asked.

"I'm a psychology major."

"Not that." I sighed. "You were attacked for a reason. What makes you strange and weird?"

"I'm not weird," she shot back, offended.

Oh great, the popular girl attitude.

"Tell me," I said patiently. "Do guys come onto you all the time?"

"That's not my fault," she said frowning. "It's not like I ask for it. I don't even like the attention."

"Do you find that when you ask for things, people just comply with what you want?"

"I'm a nice girl," she insisted.

Amaymon rolled on all fours and let out a screech. "Oh, for chrissakes, get on with it, man. This is worse than the acting in porn movies." He turned his little feline head toward her. "You're a succubus."

Amaymon, master of subtlety.

"I'm a what?" she asked.

"I was easing into it," I told him.

"Easing into it?" he echoed exasperatedly. "No wonder you never get laid."

"I'm a what?" she repeated.

"I was trying to use tact," I insisted. "Ever heard of it?"

"Dude, grow a pair," he shot back.

"WHAT THE FUCK IS A SUCCUBUS?"

That got our attention.

"You're a sex demon," Amaymon said.

"Technically, half a sex demon," I added.

"You mess with people's heads to get laid."

"It's more like procreation," I said, thinking that would somehow soften the blow.

It didn't.

"You'll fully manifest when you're twenty," Amaymon said.

"Which is plenty of time to learn how to control yourself," I reassured her.

The cat snickered. "And grow a good rack."

"Your rack is absolutely-" I started before catching myself and glaring at the cat. "Dude!"

"What?"

I looked at Abigail, who crossed her arms self-consciously. Truth be told, she didn't look like the supermodel your mind automatically conjures up when you think 'succubus'.

She was petite and slim, and she was sexy, in that girl-next-door sort of way. A good mix between hot and nerdy if you ask me. But no, she wasn't getting any double takes on the street.

Maybe at comic con.

"You don't say that to a girl," I berated the cat. "She's very pretty and you should apologize."

When the heck did I become the gentleman?

Amaymon snickered. "Erik, are you into the shy-but-cute type? Or do you just like lolitas?"

I grabbed the cat by the collar.

"That's it. Time out for you," I said, flinging the cat over my shoulder and sending him sailing over the couch.

I turned back to Abigail, who sat there with a very confused look on her face.

"Ignore everything he said," I said placing my hands together. "Yes, you're a succubus."

"Is it true what he said about the sex?"

"Yes. Your power stimulates the part of the brain that's

responsible for raw emotion, particularly lust. Fully mature succubii use this power to mate and procreate. It's also their source of feeding."

"I'm a sex vampire?" she asked incredulously.

"In a way. Except you guys leech off energy rather than blood."

She set the coffee cup down. "Why?"

"It's usually a hereditary thing," I replied.

"I was raised in a foster home."

That explains it. Succubii and incubii weren't exactly model parents. They nursed children for about a week before leaving them with the authorities for adoption or under state control.

Abigail began crying. Hell, I would have cried too. A poor, innocent girl was going to become a monster and there wasn't jack anyone could do.

Unless…

"There's still hope," I said. She looked up. "Your powers won't start affecting you until you're twenty."

"I'm nineteen," she said.

"I know. Which is why it's not too late."

"For what?"

I sighed. "To train yourself. To control your mind and your powers. It is theoretically possible to feed without killing or impregnating yourself. It's a matter of control."

"How do I do that?" she asked.

"I can help with some training," I said. "But this isn't gonna be easy. And even if you manage, you'll still be a succubus. You'll still have to feed. It's your nature."

"But I won't kill? I'll still have a life?"

"Yes. Theoretically," I insisted.

"Okay. I'm ready."

"Hold up." Amaymon hopped back on the couch. "Aren't you forgetting something? Like Gil and angels chasing after her? Not to mention whatever sent her to the hospital."

"Okay, then. We find a place to lay low until we can figure out what exactly is after her," I replied.

"And then what, genius?" Amaymon shot back. "Let both your sister and the big bad monster duke it out and take out whoever is left?"

"Sounds like a plan."

"One problem. Right now that chick is hot and I don't mean that in the good way. Every monster is gonna be after her." He rubbed against her legs. "Not to mention the guys who are gonna chase after her. She's practically jailbait."

Abigail's face twisted in disgust and kicked the cat away.

"How do you live with him?" she asked.

"I constantly ask myself that same question," I replied. "But he does have a point."

She glared at me.

"Not about the jailbait thing," I quickly added. "But your powers may flare up again."

"And that is why you keep me around. I solve problems," said the cat.

"You also create them," I murmured.

Amaymon ignored me. "Have you thought of where we can go into hiding?" He took one look at my blank expression and shook his head. "Wait here."

The cat darted up the stairs and disappeared.

"Is that a good thing?" Abigail asked.

"Hell no."

Amaymon returned with a pamphlet in his mouth. "We can go here."

I took the glossy paper and frowned.

"A cruise? You want us to go on a cruise?"

As far as dumb ideas went, this one was slowly creeping into first place.

"Why not?"

"How is that going to help us?" I asked, practically yelling.

Amaymon hissed in annoyance. "It's a constantly moving location which makes scrying a real bitch. The water dissipates the flow of magic so summoning is out of the question. And take a look at yourself."

"What's wrong with me?"

"Lots of things but mainly you do not belong on a classy ship like that. Which is why it's the last place anyone would look for *you*," he said. I did not appreciate the emphasis on that last point. "This is not an idea you would have, which is precisely what will throw Gil off."

I frowned.

Truth be told, I couldn't find anything wrong with what he said. It was true that water messed with magic and a moving target was ideal.

Since when did the cat become the brains of the operation?

"And I haven't even gotten to the best part," he continued. "It's a singles' cruise."

"So?"

"So that means there's gonna be a whole bunch of lonely, horny people trolling the decks for other lonely, horny people. The whole thing is gonna be one giant orgy," he explained, practically oozing out joy. "And what better place for someone whose constantly leaking sexual energy to hide? It'd be like trying to find a needle in a giant pile of needles."

"And how do we pay for this?" I asked.

"Gil's payment for the Behemoth job, Gracie's check and the money for the lizardmen job. That should cover the week," he promptly replied.

"You seem to have given this a lot of thought," I commented.

"I'm a pervert, Erik," he replied simply. "I keep an eye out for potential hunting grounds."

At least he was honest about his motives. Forget saving the girl—the demon just wanted to sink in debauchery.

I turned to Abigail. "What about you? How do you feel about all this?"

"Very confused," she replied.

"I mean, will you be able to control yourself?" I emphasized. "It's gonna be an open buffet, especially for someone like you."

She shook her head. "I have no choice."

And she was right.

She had no choice in the matter. This was a frying pan or fire situation. At least on the ship I could keep an eye on her. If she just fed off the residual energy, that's one thing. Worst case scenario would be if she started humping people out of their lives.

Literally.

"Okay," I said finally. "Ground rules."

I turned to Abigail. "You stay with me at all times. If you feel urges of any kind, no matter how wild or embarrassing, you tell me. Don't let it build up and do something stupid. And you," I said turning to the cat. "Are cat's even allowed on board?"

"Nope," Amaymon replied flatly.

I sighed. Nothing was ever easy.

"So, here's how it's gonna work," I said. "You do not leave my side either but keep an eye out for any demons. Or my sister. And most of all, you *do not* talk to other passengers. At all. Got it?"

He raised a paw. "Aye, aye, Captain."

I looked the leaflet over again. Might as well make this a working vacation.

"Go to the store and get a change of clothes," I told Abigail handing her some cash. "I'll pack whatever I need and meet you guys back here in half an hour."

I attached the ruby to Amaymon. "Keep an eye on her," I said. "And don't be late."

Once they left I proceeded to stuff a gym bag with whatever I thought I would need. Ammo, crystals, some potion ingredients in case I had to play chemist, and some clothes.

I looked around and sighed for the hundredth time that

day. Even if I came back in one piece, I still had an office to rebuild. Hell, maybe I'll just bill Gil for it. It was on her orders that Jack attacked me in the first place.

Abigail soon reappeared with four stuffed bags. Sending her shopping with a roll of cash and a demon for company was an amateur mistake on my part.

Amaymon winked at me. "Nothing like helping out a girl with her shopping to make her like you."

The joke was on him—that money was coming out of his cat food.

Chapter 14

I had a plan.

It was a simple plan but I *had* a plan. I would walk up to their office, buy tickets and get on the boat.

Simple, right?

We spent three days hopping from one motel to another. I taught Abigail some basics on controlling her energy flow, so she wasn't constantly sending out strong magical signals.

But it wasn't foolproof.

The most important thing for us now was getting on that boat.

When I told Amaymon my plan, he laughed in my face, before explaining in explicit detail just how dumb I was and how one can't simply buy tickets to such a thing. Apparently you have to check for availability; the one tiny detail I had overlooked.

Then, he suggested a sure fire way to get on the boat without technically breaking any rules.

"Use the girl," he said.

When I glared at him, he elaborated.

"You can't force your way through. I mean, *you* can," he said looking at me. "But then you would whine about how bad a decision that was and give me a headache. You need someone to mess with their heads, to make them do your bidding, and Abigail over here is the perfect person to do so."

I waved him quiet. "So, you want her to seduce whoever is in charge into signing our names down?"

"Yes."

"Doesn't that strike you as immoral?"

"Ah, yes," he replied sarcastically. "Immoral. I'm sure if you explained that nicely to your sister and her angels she'll call off the chase. What's her number again?"

"I get it, I get it," I said.

And that was the end of that particular conversation.

We parked outside their office the following day and went over our game plan.

"All I need is for them to be a little fuzzy," I instructed Abigail. "Think you can cover that?"

I intended to do most of the talking, anyway.

Amaymon had other ideas.

"Hey, what kinda car do you drive?" he asked Abigail.

She looked at him quizzically. "A Lexus convertible. Why?"

"Figures," he replied. "Are you loaded?"

"What? No. I got it at a good price," she said defensively.

"Uh-huh," said the cat.

"What are you getting at, Amaymon?" I asked.

"She charmed the dealer," he replied flatly.

"No, I did not!" she retorted.

"How did you feel when you talked to the guy? When you got the car?" he asked.

Abigail shook her head. "I don't know. Happy?" she suggested.

"Of course, happy," he replied. If cats could roll their eyes, he would have. "Look deeper."

"I don't know."

Amaymon stood on all fours and climbed onto her lap. "You felt in control. Euphoric. You felt like you were a dominating force and had control over anything."

Abigail swallowed hard. "I - I'm not sure. I might have. How do you know all this?"

Amaymon purred. "I'm a demon, too, girl. That's how we roll." He flicked his tail and rubbed his head with his front paw before sitting down elegantly on her lap.

"Listen to me. You and I are both demons. Sure, yeah, I'm a full demon older than Earth itself and you're a genetic mix between demon and human, but our fundamental nature is the same."

He stared intently up at her. "We get our powers from chaos. It's our nature."

She stared back down at him, as if in a trance.

"If you're trying to make a point, just spit it out, Amaymon. We're on a schedule," I said.

Amaymon flicked his ear irritably. "Okay, here's the key. What is the one thing that makes humans so chaotic?" he asked as he alternated his gaze between the two humans in the car.

Neither of us had any idea what he was talking about.

"Emotions!" he yelled exasperatedly after a few seconds. "Holy kittens, how did you ever make it as a species?"

He let out an exaggerated sigh.

"Tap into those emotions," he told Abigail. "Dominate, control. I want you to walk in there like you own the place and everyone in it, got it?"

"Are you sure?" she asked.

"He might be onto something here," I said. "But I still don't want you to go overboard with it. Just let me do the talking, okay?"

She nodded, but I could tell she was still unsure.

That made two of us.

We entered the office and it was clear which of us was in control. Abigail's stride suggested a profession where cameras flash, fans swoon, and salaries are well above the six zeros figure. She walked in front of me, her pose almost suggesting that she was blessing each tile by stepping over it. She reached the counter and looked at the guy behind the desk. He was completely lost in her gaze. She said something and made delicate movements with her hands. There was a subliminal sway of her body which made everyone's brain stop working, mine included.

The poor guy behind the desk never stood a chance.

We were offered coffee. Heck, I didn't even know this place gave you coffee—no one else had any.

There was one guy who kept passing by our desk. I guess

he was trying to burn her image into his skull. I really hoped he'd be alright. Lust over a fantasy has driven one too many men over the edge, even without magical enhancement.

I had managed to resist her charm but that didn't mean I was out of it just yet.

Let's just say that walking became very awkward.

I let her do the talking. Anything I would say would sound like white noise at this point. Instead, I used the time to reflect on something.

This was some serious power she had. I doubt even one person in the building was unaffected by her.

And she was only a budding succubus, not even at full power yet. Just how strong will she get once she's fully mature?

That thought was immediately followed by, *if she goes rogue, will I be able to take her down?*

What scared me most was that right that second, I didn't have a clear answer.

The deal was done and a few minutes later, Abigail and I were the happy couple with the Imperial Suite.

But even when we stepped outside, she did not drop her glamour.

"Abigail?"

She turned and the brunt of her power was aimed at the only other person there: me.

"What?" she whispered in a tone that made me fantasize about very depraving things starring the two of us. Her hand snaked onto my shoulder and suddenly I couldn't breathe.

A split second later, Dark Erik showed up again, like a

Deus Ex Machina. I felt my power push against hers. Still, I have to admit that I only made it out because she was still a novice and had little to no control over her abilities.

I grabbed her shoulders firmly and hugged her. She yelped in surprise but I didn't care.

I know what you're thinking but no, I did not give in to her influence. I simply just needed her within the range of my aura. I fired off a spell aimed directly at us. The tempcrature plummeted so violently, it was painful. Snow formed around us as the moisture in the air crystalized.

We both jumped away from each other, the frost congealing away any fantasy or depravity going on in our minds. It was the mother of all cold showers but it did the trick.

We stood there for a minute, panting at one another, and she refused to meet my eyes.

"It's normal," I said after a while.

Abigail gave me a reproachful look, with none of that confidence she had when we walked inside the office building.

"I'd be more worried if you weren't attracted to power," I insisted.

"How so?" Her voice was a whisper but there was nothing sensual about it.

I smiled at her. "Because then you wouldn't be human," I said reassuringly. She nodded understandingly and opened the car door.

She still couldn't meet my eyes.

Amaymon's head popped from the car. "Did I miss anything?"

Chapter 15

They say you never know how big something is until you see it up close.

On the other hand, if you can see something from forty-five minutes of road away, my guess was it's big enough. As we got closer to the ship I lost count of how many times I wondered how such a gargantuan hunk of metal could float.

We walked up the carpeted gangplank-like thing where members of staff in sailor's uniforms welcomed passengers. Abigail showed them our tickets and once again I saw loopy smiles on their faces. Naturally they completely ignored yours truly, which was fine by me.

I get enough stares back home.

Besides, I had some stuff in my gym bag which I was pretty sure not allowed in any public place.

As soon as we were alone in our room, my gym bag began shaking violently.

"Erik," came Amaymon's muffled voice from inside. "I know we're alone now. Let me out."

The cat struggled inside the gym bag.

We could only manage to afford two tickets, so Amaymon had to be stuffed inside the bag with my belongings and snuck aboard as a cat. He had made some obvious pun about the cat being literally inside the bag and complied. I think he was actually looking forward to it.

And as the victim of most of his pranks, it was my duty to make him regret that decision.

I chucked the bag on the king-sized bed and just watched the show. It was like something out of a cartoon as the bag hopped from side to side.

"The all-powerful Amaymon, brought down by the mighty zipper," I said as Abigail stifled a laugh and joined me in watching the struggle. We began giggling like idiots.

"Erik! Let me out of this damn bag!"

Nah, not yet. It's not every day I get to screw the cat over.

"I swear to God, Erik, if you don't let me out of here I am going to mark my territory over everything inside here. Let me out of this bag, you son of a bitch," he yelled from the bag. Then he went quiet.

The damn cat was pissing on my equipment.

I rushed over and unzipped the bag, freeing the cat inside.

"Good one," Amaymon said. "That makes our tally one for you and a million for me."

I chuckled proudly.

"I'm starting to think you guys are a bunch of idiots," Abigail said as she rummaged inside her own bag. She pulled out a colorful article of clothing and waved it in my face. "I am going to go change. Don't let him peep," she said, pointing at the cat.

Amaymon scoffed at her. "I can only imagine the hot babes here. Who would waste time on you, little girl?"

A pillow sailed across the room and hit the cat.

"Can you not be disgusting for a second?" I asked him as I checked to make sure none of my stuff smelled like cat urine.

"I lick myself clean," he replied. "What do you think?"

Before I could come up with an answer, the phone rang. "Hello?"

There was a breath on the other side and a soft chuckle. "Hello, brother."

Oh, crap.

"Oh, crap." I'm not one to hide my feelings.

"How are you enjoying your stay?" Gil smoothly asked from the other end.

"How did you find me?"

"Painstakingly," she replied. "We have to meet."

"I disagree," I said and prepared to hang up on her.

"The angels agreed to talk," I heard her say.

Did I say 'oh, crap' already?

I held the receiver very firmly to my ear. "What changed?"

"Everything." Way to be ominous, Gil.

She sighed. "Meet me at the pool once we leave port. That should be in about three hours. Don't be late," she ordered before hanging up.

I remained there for another couple of seconds, listening

to the dial tone as if it could provide some answer which didn't make my head feel like exploding.

That was a lot to ask out of a dial tone.

"Gil?" asked the cat as he curled up on the bed. Clearly, he had been eavesdropping on our conversation.

"Gil," I confirmed.

"If angels agreed to spill information, then that's a good thing, right? Might shed some light on our mystery," he said as he bent over and began licking his leg.

"Yeah. We still gotta figure out what attacked the girl in the first place, and why," I said as I began absentmindedly pacing around the room. "And can you please not do that when I'm around?"

Amaymon released the hold on his leg, and whistled. "Check out the babe."

I spun and saw Abigail exit the bathroom wearing a colorful bikini, which inspired equally colorful fantasies. She also had one of those sarong things around her waist which hugged her body in all the right places.

"You alright?" she asked me.

I was staring at her—of course I was staring at her! I was just a guy and she, a very attractive succubus.

Get a grip, Erik. You're on a job here.

I shook myself out of my trance.

"Yeah. Yeah," I said.

"Who was that on the phone?" she asked.

"Gil."

Abigail raised an eyebrow.

"Gil is my sister. You remember her. She had a demon

dog and threw a lot of spells at me and wanted to kidnap you," I explained.

"Was that before or after *you* kidnapped me?" she asked sarcastically.

Amaymon let out a chuckle. "She's got you there, dude."

"It was a rescue," I insisted. "Proof of that is you're here on a cruise ship in a bikini rather than in a dungeon with a straightjacket." Some people can be really ungrateful. "By the way, why are you wearing a bikini?"

Her eyebrows shot up. "I'm going for an interview with the CEO of Disney," she replied sarcastically.

"I'll take a piece of that sexy princess," muttered the cat.

Abigail made a gagging sound.

"I saw a pool the size of my high school gym," she said flatly. "I am going swimming before whatever is after me catches up and kills me."

I made for my bag and rummaged for a change of clothes.

"Fine. We got to meet Gil there either way," I said. "I'm coming with you."

"Hey, they have lobster here," Amaymon yelled. "I wanna find a place and clean 'em out."

He wasn't joking. The guy could bankrupt a fast-food chain in a single night.

I got changed and attached Amaymon's pendant to his collar. I caught a glimpse of myself in the mirror—swimming trunks, tank top and flip-flops. I looked like the tourist archetype. Unless you noticed the short sword wrapped in my beach towel and Amaymon's eyes. Then it was goodbye Fun Land and hello Horrorville.

Abigail stood at the door with her hands on her hips. "Are you going to chaperone every move I make?"

"Yes. Unless you have a death wish."

"It's broad daylight," she said exasperatedly. "Every time I felt like I was being chased, it was at night. I mean, we're on a huge ship full of people. Relax for a second will you?"

Ah, there it was. Defiance and ego weren't a good mix.

Little Miss Succubus thought she was safe just because the sun happened to be up. She thought a crowd of tourists were going to keep her safe. Perhaps she thought herself powerful enough to control everything and everyone.

What a freaking idiot.

"So, you think you're okay on your own?" I asked.

She shrugged. "I don't see any danger. And I can take care of myself."

"Okay," I said. Time to show some tough love. I cocked my head slightly, in the cat's direction. "Amaymon."

The cat disappeared.

Amaymon, in his human form, leaned against the door, rubbing shoulders with her. Then he pushed. It wasn't a hard push—just the strength it took for a person to press a button, but Abigail was sent flying across the cabin and tumbled painfully.

"Whatever is chasing you is not human," I said menacingly. She gave me a horrified look, one which I ignored.

Tough love, Erik. Tough love.

"They're probably around Amaymon's level of power," I said. "So, if you can deal with him, you're free to do whatever you wanna do."

The demon hissed and bared his fangs. As he slowly walked toward her, his clawed fingers raked the air.

Then I tapped his shoulder and stopped him.

"But that may not be the case. Most likely there is someone pulling their strings," I said. "Like an evil wizard."

I dropped my towel and sword, and approached her.

"So, here's your chance," I challenged. "Charm me and make me call him off."

The succubus got to her feet. I could feel her power flow from her body, like a heater left on for too long.

"You're mine," she growled.

I felt her power hit me and I actually stumbled. But I was ready for her.

I used her power to fuel mine and my own aura flared. I might not be able to use magic, and I may not be the most competent wizard around, but if there was one thing I never lost at it was a cock fight.

I had more raw power than most creatures I met. Even Amaymon recoiled when I cut loose, and he was as badass as they came. My energy reserves were so large that I could automatically heal from one death blow after another. My magic rendered me virtually immortal, and this little girl thought she could go toe-to-toe with me.

My energy release actually drove her to her knees. I heard a faint scream escape her and she began shaking as I approached.

I knelt next to her and allowed my aura to recede. The lesson was over.

"I know you're scared," I told her gently. Tears flowed from her eyes. "I know this is a very scary world you've just stepped into and you don't get half of what's going on." I gently grabbed her hand. "You're not as helpless as you think you are, but you can't deal with these guys. This is way out of your league."

Then I smiled, the same way my own teacher smiled when he saved my life. "But that's okay. We all need help once in a while. There's no shame in asking for it."

I helped her up and handed her a tissue. "I'm sorry for what just happened," I said.

It was true. I hated having to rough people up and I especially hated making women cry. But it was either this, or watch her get killed.

"We're on your side, Abigail," I reassured her. "I promise you, I will not let anyone or anything harm you. But you have to trust me."

She hung her head.

"I need to get stronger," she managed after a while. "Stronger and better. More control. I need to control this thing inside me." She tried a weak smile.

"Control is good. Good judgment is good, too," I said.

She nodded. "I won't be a pain again."

"And I won't be such a douche," I replied.

We both looked at Amaymon.

"Hey, he made me do it," he said innocently. "I'm a victim here."

It wasn't very convincing, especially with that grin of his and the villainous chuckle that followed.

"Come on," I said as I rolled my eyes. "Let's go for that swim."

Right before I followed Abigail out of the cabin I heard Amaymon mutter, "Hot babes and all the family comedy I could use. Man, I'm lovin' this already."

Chapter 16

I can't remember the last time I went on vacation. Probably because I've never been on vacation. Hunting supernatural monsters doesn't exactly pay well.

Abigail was in the pool and, as usual, every person there was giving her way too much attention. Amaymon had settled at the bar and I really didn't want to know what he was up to. He could be spiking people's drinks for all I cared. He kept giggling as he watched people rushing to the bathroom.

Hey, we all have our hobbies.

I guess he got bored after a while because he came over to the deck chair I was lounging on and handed me a beer.

"Why'd you do that?" I asked weakly.

He slumped down next to me. "It amuses me."

Our bottles clinked.

"So, what time did your sister say she's gonna meet you?"

"Should be in about an hour," I replied.

But of course, Gil has her own timing.

Her shadow cast over me and I opened my eyes to find her looming over me, wearing a summer dress and a pair of designer sunglasses that probably cost more than my car. Her platinum blonde hair glimmered under the sunlight.

"Hello, brother," she said.

"I think you meant one minute," Amaymon quipped.

I sat up and made sure Djinn was still within reach. Hidden, but within reach.

Abigail got out of the pool and approached us. I held my hand out and stopped her a few feet away from us.

"No tricks," I told Gil.

She held up her right arm. "No tricks," she said, rolling her eyes. "Scout's honor."

I was about to point out that she was never in a Scout group, when Mephisto beat me to the punch.

"Isn't this pleasant?" he said.

Even on the ship, Mephisto was wearing his butler suit. Behind him I saw Gil's two angel flunkies in their FBI uniforms, and from far away you could almost mistake them for bodyguards.

That would make my sister the celebrity. She certainly looked the part.

"Why you gotta bring him here?" Amaymon complained. He was still lying on the deckchair, completely ignoring the arrival of either my sister, his brother or the angels. Instead, he just belched loudly.

"Brother," Mephisto replied. "I could smell you from all the way ashore."

"Don't piss me off, asshole. Last time I checked I can still kick your ass," Amaymon shot back.

"Mere luck."

"You wanna have another go?"

Gil stepped in front of her familiar.

"This is too much testosterone for my taste," she said before turning to Abigail. "Hi, I'm Gil. So sorry we didn't properly introduce ourselves last time."

Abigail glared at her outstretched hand and recoiled.

Gil sighed. "Well, I guess there are some hard feelings after all."

I crossed my arms. "So. Why are we meeting here?"

Gil smiled. "Because it turns out we are both after the same thing."

"You're not taking the girl," I insisted.

Gil let out a bark of laughter. "Keep your precious succubus, Erik," she said. "I was referring to what is hunting her."

"Huh. And what would that be?" I asked.

A buzzing sound penetrated my head, like a faulty radio station struggling to get a clear signal.

Not here, a voice rang in my head. It sounded exactly like the voice in my dream, the one that led me to Abigail and the start of this whole case.

The angels, I thought. The sense of urgency I got from them told me they were about to share some seriously classified information—the apocalyptic kind.

To hell with it. I was comfortable here, out in the open, where I had the advantage. No way was I trusting them.

"No, I'm thinking here is just fine," I said. The buzzing

stopped. "You guys better start speaking english because we are *not* having this conversation in white noise."

"The information is too sensitive to be divulged freely."

So, they could speak english.

It was the one on the right who spoke, in that robotic way which reminded me of a badly edited sci-fi movie. They didn't ever move their stiff necks and only their lips went up and down.

"Well, tough shit," I said. "You can either accept my terms or go back to whatever shit hole you came out of. Let your imaginary god listen to your whining."

You know how you hear yourself say something and you know it's wrong but you just can't stop yourself? I've mouthed off people in the past and suffered repercussions. But these guys took that to a whole new level.

The angels glowed brighter and brighter, like a pair of suns going supernova.

"Speak not your Lord's name in vain." Their voices were like a megaphone in my head.

Gil stepped in between us. "Zamiel, Escariel. There is no need for such drastic actions. He meant nothing by it." She was actually sweating.

"The heathen must die for his actions," said one of them.

Amaymon hopped to his feet. "Alright! It's been a while since I fucked up an angel. Let's rock."

"Enough, both of you," Gil yelled. "Erik, control your familiar." Her magical aura flared.

"You need him," she growled at the angels. "Think of the priorities."

She actually got through to them and their glowing receded.

Gil glared at me as she panted. "How about you do not anger the celestial beings?"

"How about a new rule?" I suggested, talking directly to the angels. "No one fights, and we all go home in one piece. What do you say?"

They nodded very slowly.

"I could have taken them," Amaymon murmured. He sat down and actually sulked.

"Okay, then," I said. "Let's hear it. What's after Abigail?"

Both of them twisted their heads to look at each other. The edges of their sunglasses glowed like the corona around a sun during a solar eclipse. When they finally spoke their voice was one.

"Lust."

I stared at Gil, who had an equally befuddled expression on her face.

"Come again?" I asked.

"The Seven have taken physical manifestation," they said.

I looked around. Maybe the others understood what was happening. Gil and Abigail just stared at the angels, waiting for the next clue.

Good; for once I wasn't the only one not getting it.

Mephisto and Amaymon simultaneously let out a quick bark of laughter, something which I took as a very bad omen.

"The Seven?" I asked. "Seven what? Stars? Sisters? Cute little kittens? I bet it's not cute little kittens."

"Try the Seven Deadly Sins," Amaymon said with a lopsided smile. "Pride, Greed, Sloth, Wrath, Gluttony, Lust, and Envy."

"Why can't it ever be kittens?"

"The Seven Deadly Sins?" Gil asked. "I thought they were just biblical symbols. Please, explain."

"They are, Master Gil," Mephisto replied. "They are simply a categorization of different ways humans fall. Essentially just an elaborate list, nothing more."

"Then, what the hell are you guys on?" I asked, poking a finger at the angels.

They did that weird robotic thing again, where they moved their heads together to look at me.

"The Seven Deadly Sins are a categorization of human temptation. They are fueled by human energy despite being demonic in nature," they said.

"And what's that got to do with everything?"

"The Sins are energy, the foulest and most negative energy of all," explained the angels. "Now, they have been assimilated with certain high-level demons, giving the Sins a physical form."

"Ah, come on," Amaymon countered. "You got any idea what sort of power that would take to make something that abstract into a reality?"

The angels looked at him. "It would take far more power than all of us present here put together."

"So, it's god-like power?" Abigail asked, speaking for the first time.

"Your assimilation is not incorrect," they replied.

"Oh, so that's what we're dealing with here?" I said. "An evil god who created seven super demons. So, why chase after Abigail?"

"We do not know."

"Any idea what they want?"

"We do not know," they repeated.

This was getting irritating. "What *do* you know?"

"If the Sins are allowed to roam free, then this plane will no longer be in equilibrium. Evil will reign and this world will become a second Hell," said the angels.

"Hey, don't knock it," joked my familiar. "We throw great parties."

"Under no circumstances is the balance to tip over," they continued. "We will send an envoy, a Virtue who may counter the Sin, in order to preserve balance."

"An envoy?" I echoed.

That didn't sound right. It looked to me like they were trying to do us a favor and make us owe them. And these guys were sure to come collect.

That's how invasions usually start.

"What if we reject this envoy?" I asked.

Everyone turned to look at me, but I kept my eyes fixed on the angels. This conversation was feeling more and more like a Mexican standoff.

"Then, the Sin of Lust will win and the world will be that much closer to ending. If one Sin is allowed to spread its corruption, it will be easy for the following Sins to spread as well. It is time to choose, Erik Ashendale, between your stubborn pride and the fate of the world."

Ouch. Schooled by an angel.

"That is all we can divulge."

They shimmered for a minute and then just froze. It was as if someone had pressed the reboot button on these guys, and a split second later, both of them fell silent again.

"I don't like this," I said.

"Which part?" Gil asked. "The unknown enemy or the waiting?"

"There must be something we're overlooking," I continued. "The angels said the Sin needs a demon to host it, right?"

She nodded.

"Then, it makes sense to have a demon compatible with the Sin."

"Just like when creating a channel," she said knowingly.

"Exactly," I said. "So, we gotta figure out which demon is most compatible with Lust. Kill the host, kill the Sin. Right?"

"Theoretically it makes sense," Gil agreed.

"Could it be another succubus?" Abigail suggested.

"Nah, I'd smell her from a mile away," Amaymon said.

"Yes. The demon will be ancient and powerful," Mephisto added. "Something terribly powerful, even without the Sin's power."

"I can only think of one legend that fits that description," Gil said. "Lilith."

"The Mother of all Demons," Mephisto growled.

The two demons hissed and tensed up.

"Lilith?" I asked. "Anyone care to fill me in?"

"She is known as the Mother of all Demons," Gil explained. "According to the legends, she ruled paradise and was cast down into the darkness when she became too lustful and rebellious. She gave birth to the Alphas, the ancestors of most of today's demons. Legend says that all demons are related to Lilith and she alone populated Hell."

"Is that true?" I asked Amaymon.

He nodded. "Before she came along, Hell wasn't even the Hell you know. It was just a nascent place and we were still forming it. Then, she came along and a horde followed in her wake." He bared his fangs in a smile. "They were no match for us of course, but after a while we learned to coexist. Hell was formed and the rest is history."

"We also know her as the First," Mephisto added.

"The first what?" I asked.

He gave me a significant look. "*The* First," he stressed.

I understood him then. Lilith, the first person to walk the Earth. The first human, or maybe one of our distant cousins. The first one to fall into the dark side.

Lilith—God's firstborn.

And judging by the stories told, the first woman ever scorned.

"So, we are up against the motherlode." I sighed at my own pun. "Quite literally."

I slumped back down on my deck chair and found my beer. It had gone warm by now.

"How do I beat her?" I looked around, hoping that between the two ancient demons and my genius twin sister, someone could provide me with a tangible answer.

That was all I needed right now. I was a hunter through and through—show me a monster's weakness and I'll bring back a corpse.

Gil withdrew inside her own head, probably recalling every detail she had ever read on the subject. Mephisto's expression was blank and cold like a sheet of ice. Amaymon scratched his head absentmindedly, something he only did when genuinely worried.

That, more than anything, sent me spiraling downwards.

Amaymon was a rock. He never got nervous or worried about anything. He was just that powerful. If this demon was worrying *him*, then *my* chances of survival were slim to none.

"This ain't your run-of-the-mill demon, Erik," he said without his usual swagger.

"I know," I snapped. "Just tell me, what is she?"

Mephisto cleared his throat. "That is still unknown to us. But she is capable of magic, even creation. Perhaps an ancient, purer form of the human prototype?"

"Or perhaps the people in chapter one of the Bible ain't people after all," Amaymon suggested, "but some sorta gods."

"That would explain the *god-like* power," Gil agreed.

I cringed on the inside and felt sick to my stomach.

Let's recap, shall we?

God-like woman gets thrown out of Heaven and populates Hell in revenge. Then, she gets her hands on the sin of Lust, or creates the damn thing, and schlepps over here to dominate us all.

Here was how I felt about all this: "Fuck."

"Amen, brother," Amaymon said.

"Erik," Gil said. "Wait for the Virtue. Don't do anything stupid by yourself."

"Okay," I heard myself say, even though I had absolutely no intention of doing that, and my sister knew it.

This monster had to be repelled by Earth's forces, not Heaven's. We couldn't be in their debt. That was one check the world couldn't cash.

After a few minutes of uncomfortable silence my sister and her squad of misfits left, leaving me to contend with my own squad of sorry misfits.

"You do realize there's no way I'm letting some angel save the day?" I directed at the two next to me. "If we owed them a favor, we'd be inviting them to take over."

"Thought you might say that," Amaymon said.

I sat back on my deck chair and let out the longest sigh I could muster. Abigail settled on the deck chair next to mine.

"I keep my promises," I said. I turned my head, meeting her eyes. "Remember what I promised in the cabin. I won't let you get hurt. And I always keep my promises."

"It's a demonic *god*, Erik." Her tone sounded like someone who had given up.

"If there's one thing I learned in this world," I said, "it is that no one is invincible. And the higher they think they are, the bigger the cracks in their armor."

"So, I'm assumin' you got a game plan?" Amaymon asked.

"Not yet." I got up. "Thought I might cool off for a while."

"If you're gonna drown yourself, the water ain't deep enough," he said.

"Funny."

Abigail sat up. "Want some company?" she offered.

I shook my head. "I need some time to think."

"That might take hours," Amaymon shot back.

I flipped him off and walked into the pool. Cool water surround me and I dove under, enjoying the sensation. It was like being in a sensory deprivation chamber and I was finally alone with my thoughts.

There, where I knew no one could see me, I let all the fear inside me go and screamed my lungs out.

I don't know for how long I swam and dove and screamed, but I do know that once I had gone past the fear, my brain started working again. And in that moment of clarity, a plan had formed.

I smiled.

The time for self-pity was over. I had a god to kill.

Chapter 17

We spent the rest of the day following Abigail around as she flitted from one gift shop to another. Amaymon had finally dragged us to the games room where we shot pixelated zombies with toy guns that responded badly to quick reflexes.

And all this time I ran the plan over and over in my head, ironing out the kinks. It was a great plan, as far as suicidal plans went. Some might even call it genius.

You know, until you get to the suicide part.

Finally, we settled down in a restaurant and gorged ourselves, but not before Amaymon decided to address the elephant in the room.

"What's our next move?"

"We bait her," I said as I carefully cut my steak.

"That's it?" He never bothered to swallow or stop eating. "That's all you got?"

Abigail remained quiet and just buried her face behind her water glass.

"So, how do we go about doin' that?" he continued.

I jabbed my fork at Abigail. "With her."

"What?" she squealed. "Are you trying to get me killed?"

I put my cutlery down and held up my hands. "Just hear me out."

Both of them turned their attention towards me. "I don't know why, but Lilith is after Abigail, right?" I said. "So, let's give her just that. We'll provide her with bait she can't resist and then swoop in for the kill."

Amaymon raised his eyebrows. "And you think it's gonna be that easy?"

"Why not?" I retorted. "It's how we usually work, and I think now, more than ever, we should be playing to our strengths."

"And what if something goes wrong?" Abigail asked.

She was right to be scared, I suppose. She was the bait, and if something did go wrong, she would end up as monster chow.

But I wasn't seeing any other solutions.

"What if she gets to me and you guys aren't around?" she added.

"That ain't the problem," Amaymon said. "We're definitely gonna be there, and we will help you out. The only problem is that we know exactly bubkis about this demon. We don't know if we can kill it."

"I thought you were all powerful," I quipped.

"I am," he replied seriously. "But I also ain't stupid. No creature hunts something that's stronger than itself, Erik."

That stilted the conversation.

"I just can't accept that," I said after a while.

"You might not have a choice."

"NO!"

I didn't mean to shout, but I guess the stress was starting to get to me. Amaymon's eyes widened. I'd never yelled at him before, at least not about anything as serious as this.

"This case has something to do with the curse," I said. "I don't know how or why, but I can feel it."

I turned to him.

"You know as well as I do that there are no coincidences. Everything in our world happens for a reason. And here's what I know. A bunch of lizardmen take a school hostage without harming anyone. A genetically mutated lizardman shows up and decks me. Then, Gil comes along with a traitor and a busted mansion. Now, out of thin air, the Seven Deadly Sins just take form and come hunting succubii," I said as I jabbed a finger at Abigail. "Can you spell conspiracy?"

Amaymon's feline eyes narrowed. "Still doesn't answer the question. Can we take her?"

I sighed heavily. "You and I alone, probably not."

The words tasted badly in my mouth but that didn't make them any less true. Judging from the legends alone, this one was more than we could chew.

"But you're forgetting something," I added. "We are not alone. Gil, Mephisto, the angels, and whoever this Virtue is, are all on our side now. I think all of us together can stop the demon."

Amaymon said nothing. I doubt he believed me.

Demons were largely instinctual monsters. If his instincts told him to avoid this threat, then I had to make one heck of an argument to convince him otherwise. But I would deal with him later.

Besides, no matter what his instincts told him, his contract to me wouldn't allow him to just abandon me. Right now Amaymon had an internal conflict: listen to his instincts and run, or obey the terms of our contract and stay.

I left him to sort it out by himself.

"So," I said, settling back down. The steak had gone cold now, but I had lost my appetite long before it did. "We lure her out."

"When?" Abigail asked.

I pointed to a poster in response. "There's a welcoming dance tonight. Lots of people go to those things. The perfect spot for a predator to blend in."

"And what am I supposed to do?" she asked.

I smiled. "Buy a sexy dress and be the center of attention."

Her eyebrows shot up.

"Now this I'm interested in," Amaymon said with a devious grin.

"You go in, charm everyone you meet, do your… whatever it is you do, and when the Sin comes to get you, we'll keep it busy until the cavalry arrives," I instructed.

Amaymon leaned in closer to her. "Don't you worry, babe. I'll be watching your every move." He made a purring noise that sent chills down my spine.

I grabbed his ear and pulled him away. "I'll be watching

both of you," I said.

Abigail closed her eyes, sighed and grabbed Amaymon's wine glass, draining it in one go. "If I die, I swear I'll come back and haunt you forever. You will never, ever get laid again," she threatened. "Let's go."

She rose up and abruptly turned to me. "And I'm choosing the dress. No whining about the price."

I nodded.

As we got up from the table, Amaymon nudged my side. "Don't worry, you won't know the difference if she does haunt you," he said. "You still can't get laid either way."

"Wait until we get to the dress shop," I replied with a sigh. "She'll screw me without taking her clothes off."

Chapter 18

I was regretting my plan already. It was easy to say 'we'll wait and see', but actually doing it was a totally different story.

There were a couple of factors I overlooked when devising my brilliant strategy.

The first was the fact that I had to sit on my ass all night while everybody else danced and had a good time.

I settled on a stool at the bar and surveyed the crowd there. It was mostly people in their late twenties and the majority of them were in groups. They laughed and made a lot of noise, all of which made me feel very old.

And bitter.

I was only a little older than they were and already felt twice as old. I guess having to do a lot of growing up in a very short period of time does that to you.

The second thing that pissed me off was all the attention Abigail was getting.

She entered the room half an hour after me since I had to make sure I had a good feel of the room before she went in. The succubus strutted in wearing a dress that would have probably bankrupted me; a short, provocative number which was still classy enough not to give her any labels. She wore her red hair loose around her shoulders and had little makeup on.

Who needs enhancement when nature gives you all of that?

I could feel her power all the way from the entrance of the hall. Damn, the girl was strong. Just what sort of damage could she do when she fully matured? I shuddered to even think about it.

Abigail strode in and took a glass of champagne from a stunned waiter. Poor guy—she was going to be haunting his dreams for weeks to come.

She made her way to the dance floor and suddenly it was a feeding frenzy. Guys were all over her, either trying to buy her a drink or get her to dance with them. She smiled and gently rejected some of them, dancing only with the good looking ones.

I automatically hated their guts.

No, I wasn't jealous—just concerned for her.

Yeah, right. Keep drinking the cool-aid, Erik.

At the same time, Amaymon was on the opposite side of the dance floor, and clearly he was having the time of his life. I also suspected he was messing with the DJ's playlist.

Why would anyone play the Blues Brothers to a crowd born two decades after the group was famous?

At one point he even started dancing. And by dancing I mean he was doing the robot. Because clearly he did not know the meaning of the word shame.

And then, she walked in.

There should be a rule somewhere that says two breathtaking woman can't be in the same room at once. Makes it easier for us guys to acquire our target. I mean, let's face it, we're not exactly cut out for multitasking. I'm the kind of guy who has to turn off the radio when I got lost. Meanwhile, I've seen my sister answer the phone, write down a memo and simultaneously order Mephisto about. Maybe that's why she was the boss and I'm the dancing monkey.

This woman was beautiful, a walking sculpture of perfection. Her skin had an exotic tinge to it, and her straight, pitch black hair hung loose around her shoulders. Her dress was a red number which hugged her body in all the right places. She batted her eyes at me, a pair of beautiful, dark orbs that peered right into my soul.

"You do know that drinking alone goes against the whole purpose of this dance, right?" she asked.

I was too mesmerized by her cherry-colored lips to catch what she said next.

"I'm sorry?" I mumbled.

She bent her lips into a smile that nearly had me in tears.

"Is this seat taken?" she asked. "May I join you?"

Holy crap.

I felt my insides do some backflips as if I was some teenage boy on his first date. Here she was, a woman that artists lose their minds over, with beauty that can never be captured, written or drawn…

And she wanted to sit with me?

I nodded clumsily and she took a seat, ever so gracefully, on the barstool next to mine. She ordered a drink and it came in a tall glass, with three different colors layered on top of each other: pink, orange, and green. Each color reflected in her eyes as she examined her cocktail and took a sip.

She cocked her head and I realized I was staring.

"Traditionally, people tend to mingle during these events," she said. Her voice was like ethereal music.

I shrugged and licked my very dry lips. "I'm a horrible dancer," I heard myself say.

She let out a laugh. "Me, too. That, and I am not usually one for mixers."

"So, what are you doing here tonight?"

"I enjoy watching others mingle," she replied with a wink that made my southern regions stand at attention.

I took a sip of my drink, hoping for some of that fabled liquid courage.

"So, you're scouting the talent," I said.

"Indeed," she said with a slight bob of her head.

The woman raised her glass. I followed her motion and we clanged glasses.

"I'm Rose, by the way," she said, holding out her hand.

"Erik." I shook her hand briefly and actually felt sparks between us.

When did my life become a romantic comedy?

"You have beautiful eyes, Erik. Has anyone ever told you that?" Her eyelashes did a fluttering motion which made my brain flat line for two seconds.

No one had ever commented on my eyes before. They usually take one look at my disgruntled appearance and quickly change lanes. I felt the need to compliment her in return, but like I said, my brain wasn't working.

"I like your… everything."

I cringed as I heard the words come out of my mouth.

Much to my surprise she actually giggled. "Been noticing, have you?"

"I'm observant."

"Is that so?" She raised her eyebrows slightly. "Then, what can you tell me about that one over there?"

I followed her gaze.

Abigail was sandwiched between two guys, all of them gyrating and rubbing against each other, hands wandering about. Just watching it made heat rise to my face and my throat dry.

Wow—add a cameraman and some background music, and you got yourself some soft-core porn.

And yet, there was nothing I could do. No demons, no danger. All that was left was to watch the show and listen to the little green monster inside me as it fumed.

I wanted that succubus. This was supposed to be my show and I couldn't swallow down the fact that I had to be on the sidelines.

Or maybe she was messing with my head. I already knew her powers worked very well on me. It wouldn't exactly shock anyone to know I don't date much. Abigail had a way of remind me of that little fact. Mostly because her powers were inspiring fantasies in my head that would give a priest a heart attack.

Rose had changed that, by inspiring fantasies of her own. Only in her case, she actually liked me. *She* came onto me. So, if I had to choose between who I wanted to be with at that very moment, Rose took the cake. I liked the simplicity of it all. Boy meets hot girl, hot girl miraculously likes boy— it was all very Adam Sandler.

So I tore my gaze away from Abigail and her entourage, and turned back to the woman sitting next to me.

"Not my type," I said hastily.

"Liar," she replied coyly.

"Nah, seriously," I insisted. "I prefer the shy, geeky ones."

Which wasn't a lie. If a girl can quote *Star Wars* and play *Dungeons and Dragons*, I'm interested.

Rose cocked an eyebrow. "Yes, you do seem to be that type. So, what do I have to do to get your full and undivided attention, Erik?"

"Keep talking and I'll take notes," I replied.

Yeah, I can be suave. It just doesn't happen as often as I would like it to.

Her laughter rang in my ears and I felt her hand clasp mine.

"I hope it's not too forward," she said in a coy tone, as she leaned dangerously close.

"But I really like you," she continued. This time in her voice was so sensual my insides stopped fluttering and were replaced by a cheerleading squad.

"I'm not complaining," I said huskily.

She smiled and brought her face closer to mine. I could feel the warmth of her body on me. My mind got very foggy and all I could do was sit there and enjoy the feeling of her perfect body against my own.

I saw her lips parting and we kissed, delicately at first, but slowly becoming fiercer and more passionate.

The voice of reason in my head told me to think of the mission, to think of saving Abigail from any potential danger; the voice of horniness told the voice of reason to shut the hell up.

Either way I couldn't care less. I just wanted to kiss her. I needed her, as if she were all that was missing in my life. I have no idea how I managed to get up every morning without ever knowing she existed and now that I found her I needed to touch her, to be one with her.

So I just gave in. Right there and then, she had me.

The internal struggle inside my head ceased immediately within seconds of kissing Rose. Whatever influence Abigail had on me immediately evaporated and only Rose dominated my mind now. Abigail, Lust, the angels, Amaymon: they were all just echoes now.

Only Rose mattered to me and I had to sleep with her. It wasn't anything intimate. This was sex, pure and simple.

No emotions, no strings—just crazy monkey sex.

"Shall we get out of here?" I heard her ask. Judging from her tone of voice and the look in her eyes, she was thinking along the same lines. I wanted to scream yes, but was too stunned to move. Instead, I nodded and allowed her to drag me out of the room.

Chapter 19

There were moments of clarity, like when I realized we were in my cabin and on my bed. Like when I felt my sport coat and shirt being peeled off of me. My pants followed soon after. I hated the damn things anyway.

They were becoming very… restrictive.

I remembered her dress, and I remembered how nice and pretty and red it was—and how much I wanted to rip that thing off of her. I don't know how she got naked in such a short time but I wasn't complaining. I remembered being face up on the bed with her on top of me.

Again, not complaining.

Then, the warnings began. Over the years, my brain had become trained to spot stuff that was out of the ordinary and piece it all together. And throughout the entire experience, I could hear the alarms going off in my head. But it was like a bell in a vacuum. I could see the warnings flashing but just didn't know what to do with them.

Until, he intervened.

I don't know if you've ever been bitch slapped by your subconscious but it's not pretty. Dark Erik, the manifestation of my subconscious, just popped up in my head and hit the reset button. All of that influence and fogginess went away and I was left wide eyed as a beautiful, naked goddess gyrated on top of me.

She suddenly stopped and looked wildly into my eyes.

"Interesting." Her voice no longer had that melodic tone but was now cold and powerful.

I tried moving, but her hand shot out and pinned me down. It wasn't a playful gesture. She had the strength to snap my neck in two if she wanted.

Sensation rushed back into my head and I remembered everything—Rose showing up and putting some glamour on me. It must have been some powerful stuff, to keep me under for so long. She had known immediately where to go: my cabin. She also didn't strip off the dress, but instead it had simply disappeared like a handful of ash in a gust of wind.

And most bizarre of all, her eyes kept changing colors, ranging from one end of the color spectrum to the other.

Where's Abigail? I thought. *What about Amaymon and the rest? What the hell is going on?*

Rose, or whoever she was, smiled seductively. "Pity you broke free," she said. "You could have died in utter bliss."

She bent over and her hair tickled my chest. I felt her tongue streak over my collarbone and was overwhelmed with the need to be under her spell, to give in, and let her have her way with me.

I felt her swimming inside my head, slowly taking over again. But this time, Dark Erik was ready for her.

My power flared and instead of pushing her back, I was pulled deep inside her mind. For a few moments I *was* her, with access to her memories, and saw them as a series of flashes.

A man and a woman, together in a paradise, surrounded by natural beauty that could never exist in our world. Life blossomed all around them and bliss reigned.

But with life came also the darkness, and it began tempting the woman. And the more she used the darkness, the larger it grew and the more it consumed of her until she had become a pitch black version of her former self.

Seeing this, the man feared the corruption would spread. So, he called upon magic and power and cast her out of that world. She was plunged into the all-consuming abyss. Her pain, rage and sorrow were too much for her to contain, and gave rise to demons and monsters that no human could imagine without going insane.

Eons went by and the Earth flourished. She infiltrated this seedling of a world, donating darkness and hatred. Nations fell to her powers and she conquered them like a queen. She would build her paradise here, she decided.

But that wasn't enough. She wanted the original Paradise, and so ordered her temple be built tall enough to pierce the heavens. That failed miserably due to language problems.

Once she accepted that she could never return to Heaven, she took vengeance upon the natives of this plane.

She became a temptress, whispering in the ears of kings and warlords. She instigated wars that lasted throughout the ages, relishing in the hatred she created.

One of her greatest accomplishments was the betrayal of Cleopatra. That Roman had been very easy to manipulate. Almost too easy.

Her favorite was the Trojan war. She made Helen fall madly in love and told her to run away. Then, she made Helen's father go after her. Years later, she gave a certain strategist the idea for a trap and he had come up with a giant horse.

Men, always thinking bigger is better.

More flashes placed her in Victorian garb as she tempted one monarch after another. She had whispered in Cortez's ear of her attraction to violence, and he eradicated half a nation on her behalf.

She was a court member during World War I. Before the vote to go to war, she leaned very close to an influential member and flashed enough of what was beneath her dress to persuade him in all possible meanings of the word. She voted for war and everyone else followed her.

Years later she slept with a certain German soldier who also fancied himself an artist, and encouraged his twisted philosophy. He entered politics and the world experienced its second World War. She had thoroughly enjoyed herself at first, before the idiot went ahead and took all that amphetamine. No wonder he thought invading Russia was a good idea.

And then, nothing. She seemed to give up on the world.

There was already so much darkness that she had become redundant.

So she returned to Hell and waited, until her throne was usurped by the Demon Emperor.

Not to worry—she had lost interest in that as well.

Some time ago, she felt the call of someone old and powerful. There was something familiar about that voice but she could not quite place it. Age and corruption had taken their toll on her memory.

This being, neither demon nor angel, but something long lost and forgotten, had offered her power: a new purpose. She accepted the mantle of Lust. It changed her, but only superficially while her original powers had been fortified.

The mastermind wanted to wait. He wanted to enact his plan at the right time and in the meantime she had grown impatient. So, she broke off his hold and ran to the human world, eager to wreak havoc on a new scale; to make those fragile meat bags worship her again.

But first, she had to feed. With this new power came a cost, and she had to find something to quell her hunger. The succubus had been a youngling but she would have to do. Only she would suffice, for only she had the *correct* energy. To a creature like Lilith, quality always overruled quantity. She tried feeding on her many times, yet either her powers would go haywire or Heaven's agents would intervene.

But not this time, not here on this ship. The angels were far away and all that stood between her and her meal was this idiotic wizard. A cripple at that.

When her thoughts came back to the present and focused

on me, I finally saw her for what she really was.

"I am going to suck everything out of you," she moaned.

I could have laughed at the pun. Instead, I looked down and I was never happier to see I was still wearing my underwear.

"Lilith," I snarled.

Her eyes flashed red before reverting back to their usual kaleidoscope of color.

"So, you figured out who I am. Bravo," she said. "Was that you poking around in my head a few seconds ago?" She flicked an ebony strand of hair. "Whatever. There is nothing you can do now anyway."

I struggled and she pressed forwards. It was like a car had settled on my chest.

"Fragile humans," she cooed disappointingly. Her hands snaked down south and grabbed my genitals. "But you are quite something, aren't you? I figured we'd at least get to second base before you figured it all out."

She gave my thigh a squeeze. "But I suppose this is better. I always enjoy playing with my food." She trailed kisses across my chest. "Say my name again."

I felt her hold recede just a millimeter, just enough for me to swing my fist at her.

"Go blow yourself," I spat.

She didn't dodge or even flinch. Instead, she swatted my arm away and giggled. I felt searing, white-hot pain in my arm and saw it dangling over the edge of the bed, misshapen and swollen.

"Wrong answer," she said sharply. Her hand squeezed

my genitals harder. "Shall I break another bone, my dear?"

This woman and her puns. I kept myself from saying anything. I dated her type before: insane psychos. And when that type of woman grabbed you by the balls and threatened to rip them out, you had better listen.

"Lilith," I rasped. "Your name is Lilith."

"Good boy," she whispered as she leaned over and kissed my forehead, before straightening up.

She flashed a smile. "Well, now I'm hungry, my dear."

Her perfect face began changing. Her jaws elongated and lips widened unnaturally, revealing a row of serrated fangs which dripped saliva all over me.

She may be a monster of powers way beyond mine. She may even be a goddess. Whatever she was, she was incredibly powerful, and folks with that kind of juice always make the same mistake: they underestimate the weaker guy.

I mean, sure, I've never started wars that have been made into countless movies. I certainly haven't slept with as many women as she had or had anyone drool after me. And I may also be a cripple; a wizard who cannot use magic is about as useful as swimming lessons to a cat.

But I do have a boatload of power and she underestimated me at her own expense.

My broken arm had already begun healing, and I felt magic reinforcing my body. Already I felt the pain of trying to use my powers without a channel but my options were limited.

My hand brushed against the gym bag I had stowed under the bed and felt around for the zipper. I groped around and found a cheap plastic bottle full of holy water.

Lilith swooped down and I shoved the bottle in her mouth.

"Suck on this," I spat, squeezing the bottle.

Holy water shot down her throat and she leapt backwards all the way across the room, screaming curses in an extinct language between gags. The liquid burned her flesh but her power regenerated the tissue. But take it from someone who has the same healing powers—healing doesn't mean immunity to pain.

I saw Djinn's handle sticking out from under a pile of clothes and lunged for it. Before I could grab it, a long, black nail shot out and knocked the weapon away from my reach.

Lilith's naked form rushed forwards and kicked me squarely in the chest. I was thrown backwards and into the wall. I felt ribs crack and saw a dent in the wall where my body had crashed against it.

"You men are all the same."

I felt her hand squeeze around my neck and I was lifted off my feet. "So weak," she snarled.

She drove her fists into me, again and again, systematically cracking every bone in my body.

"Why don't you all just die?"

She slapped my face so hard I heard my neck snap. A cold sensation washed over me and I just hung there like a piece of meat, fresh from the kill. My magic was working on overdrive, healing the most critical injuries first, but Lilith kept creating new ones.

Finally, she lost it.

"I'm not going to eat you," she said, grasping my hair and yanking my head up. "I'm just going to tear you to shreds and then go back to that party. I'll rip everyone apart and bring the girl back here to show her the corpse of her supposed savior. Then I'll kill her slowly while your cold, dead eyes look at us."

Her form shimmered again but I couldn't see very well. My body was slowly shutting down.

Something long, thick and disgusting slithered from her lower area. I don't want to know what it was or where it came from. It looked like a cross between an intestine and a tentacle, and it was just fucking horrible.

The appendage wrapped around me and squeezed. I felt sucker-like mouths biting into my flesh and absorbing it. The damn thing was liquefying me.

And just before the coup de grace, I heard Lilith say, "Thank you for the pick-me-up."

The appendage changed again. Thick, bony spikes, like mammoth tusks, shot out of the appendage and I felt dozens of them skewering me from all directions. And just as quickly, the spikes retracted and the bizarre appendage released me. I remembered hitting something hard, most likely the floor.

In my final moments, before darkness claimed me, I saw Lilith's naked figure walking out of the cabin and heading towards the faint music.

Chapter 20

I was dead.

Not unconscious or in some comatose state while my magic healed me.

Truly, purely, utterly *dead*.

I have seen depictions of Heaven, of a fluffy, cloudy place with lots of naked, baby angels floating around. Hell, on the other hand, was this mass of red fire, where the most stereotypical demons poked at your ass with pitchforks.

And the first thing I saw when I woke up was red.

My first thought was *crap*. Not that I would be too surprised if I did end up in Hell. Although, once you've spoken with a demon and understood the whole parallel dimension concept, the afterlife becomes kind of dull.

I felt sand in my ass and realized that I was in the middle of a desert.

Oh, right—Hell.

Everything was red. Red sand, red clouds and an amber red sky. Even the lazy gusts of wind had a reddish hue to them.

But I felt… normal. I thought only my soul would remain, or perhaps I had become a mass of quantum energy that would later be reabsorbed into the Earth's plane. Instead, I felt rough sand all over my body and the itching became too much. I scrambled up, kicking sand all over the place.

"Where the hell am I?"

Maybe 'hell' was a poor choice of word in this particular situation. But this was definitely not the afterlife, not unless some divine being was playing a really sick joke on me.

I looked down and saw that I was totally naked. Not only that, but I was also shimmering in crimson energy, as if I had a small nuclear reactor inside of me and was about to explode.

My training took over and I focused on sensing the magic around me. When in doubt, do a spot check. It helps.

At the very least it stops you from freaking out.

I felt a vast ocean of power all around me. There was no end to the magic in here. It was above and below, in front and behind, to the left and right. This place was made out of magic.

No, this place *was* magic itself. And the strangest part was that it all felt so familiar, so intimate. This magic was a part of me, living inside me and yet I had no idea it was here all along.

Or perhaps, I knew it was here all along and just refused to acknowledge it.

The curse, I thought.

I was taken back to the time when Mephisto had sat me

and Gil down and explained it all to us. That seemed like such a long time ago. It was because of that curse that our own father wanted to kill us and take all that power for himself.

And it was because of that curse that I had killed him instead. It was self-defense, but patricide wasn't something to scoff at, even under those circumstances.

It was because of that curse that I would probably never perform another spell in my life without relying on Djinn or some other channel. And it was this curse that made me heal from pretty much anything and will probably outlive anyone that mattered to me.

It was because of that curse that I was, and always will be, an outcast.

Knowing that, I denied it. I defiantly refused to explore it, or even acknowledge its existence.

So sue me. That curse only brought me pain and misery.

Then, the little voice in my head spoke out.

This was a whole lot of power down here, it said. And you did just get your ass handed to you by a demon goddess who created Hell as we know it. You might even be dead and because of that, Abigail and a whole lot of innocent people might be in serious danger.

So, how about you man the fuck up and use this power? Maybe stop bitching for ten seconds just so everyone else doesn't end up dead too?

Shut up, voice of reason.

During that little bout of schizophrenia, the world shifted. The middle of the desert parted and a large tree began growing. Its pitch black roots branched out and burrowed deep into the desert. The trunk kept growing and growing until the very top branched out and spread until it covered most of the sky. Its branches were hidden behind the clouds so I couldn't see the leaves.

Then, he emerged.

Dark Erik was just a mass of darkness at first, emerging from the trunk of the large tree. He was made from liquid obsidian and in the center of his chest, where a person's heart would be, this guy had a mass of light. Veins of red, orange and yellow snaked from the blob of light and all around the creature.

"So, you have decided to acknowledge my existence," he said.

The voice came from the entire form and echoed from all over the place. Dark Erik spoke with my voice but on a decibel level that could have shattered glass and cracked walls.

"Hey, Dark Erik," I said with a weak smile. My own voice felt weird and foreign.

Then again I guess you're bound to feel strange when conversing with the manifestation of your subconscious.

Dark Erik cocked his head. "Dark Erik," he repeated. "That is the denomination you have bestowed upon me."

My subconscious was more eloquent than I was. If I ever made it back to my office, I was going to finally read that Dickens book I'd been putting off.

Dark Erik was not amused. "How presumptuous of you to assume that I am a phantom of your mind. But I suppose that is your nature as a human."

It was my turn to cock my head. "So, are you saying that you are not a part of me?"

"I am you, and I am not you. I am one and both. I am bane and power. I am a legacy. Your legacy, Erik Ashendale."

Holy crap.

"What does all of that mean?" I asked.

Dark Erik, or whoever he was, remained silent.

"Dammit man, at least tell me your name." I probably shouldn't be pissed off at whatever he was, but hey, what could he do? I was already dead, so joke's on him.

"You have not accepted your true nature yet," he replied. "You have not even begun to grasp the significance of your destiny."

I wasn't sure whether I had a heart in my current state but something definitely skipped a beat.

"You're my curse," I whispered.

Of course, he had just said so—bane and power.

I remembered when I let that power take over during my fight with my drugged up Warlock of a father. I have nearly no memory of that event. All I know is that I had come close to dying and the curse took over. Then I woke up to find the mansion destroyed and my father nearly dissected. Whatever my curse was, it was not pretty.

But damn, was it powerful.

"Is that why I'm here?" I asked. "Is that what this place is?"

Dark Erik's form shifted and he looked around, as if seeing the place for the first time.

"It's a good thing that you are able to come here," he said. "This place is called Ashura and it's our realm, created by our magic. It *is* our magic."

Huh?

"You mean to tell me that I have an entire *world's* worth of power?" I asked incredulously.

Dark Erik let out a chuckle; my chuckle.

"I told you," he said. "I am very powerful."

"So, what am I supposed to do now?"

Dark Erik tapped me on the shoulder and we were suddenly beneath the tree. Its long, thick roots snaked all around us, shielding us like a giant mangrove cocoon.

Accept me, Erik Ashendale. The voice reverberated from the roots themselves.

"I am more powerful than the Sin," Dark Erik said. "This power is now yours, but you will be unable to use it unless you acknowledge it. Unless it becomes a part of you."

"What happens if I can't?" I asked.

Dark Erik remained silent.

We both knew the answer. Nothing would happen. I would probably dissolve into nothing and be truly gone. I would never feel the warmth of the sun or get to go home again.

I would never have another pointless conversation with Amaymon. The cat was the only true family I had. Our relationship had evolved from a strained partnership to the point where now I can actually trust him. It took a lot of time and a lot of cases, but we finally got there.

I would never see Abigail again. I would break the

promise I made to her and she would die before her powers even awakened. She would never get to live a full life and would probably die with a lot of questions still unanswered. Maybe, just maybe, I was considering taking her as a student and showing her the ropes. She might be of some help during certain cases and it would prevent her from going ballistic on some poor, horny schmuck.

And Gil—I had hoped that we would mend our relationship before one of us died. I had hoped we could be like before, back when we were close siblings trying to understand the ups and downs of magic. Before I killed our father. Before she decided to run the whole Warlock gig and made it her priority. I had hoped we could find a way to peacefully coexist. Who knows, maybe even invite each other out to lunch sometime.

Now, all of that was down the crapper and I was dead.

I felt tears running down my cheek.

I wanted to live. I never realized until now just how much I wanted to be alive and make things better.

The laughter, the hangovers, the messed up relationships; I wanted all of them back. I even wanted to continue seeing all of those things that made others go insane. I wanted to experience the true magic of life—waking up and enjoying another day in a world filled with assholes and the occasional decent person. I wanted to take on more cases like Gracie's and solve them. I wanted to bring some peace to people's hearts.

Sure, I led a life that would drive anyone off a cliff. My only upside—the magic—had so many restraints and conditions it might as well have been a legal contract.

And sure, my life was a veritable lightning rod for life's crap.

But it had been my choice, my own destiny. It had always been all my choice and I have never regretted it, not even now that I was dead.

I found myself smiling—Erik Ashendale wasn't dead, not by a long shot.

"You already know what's gonna happen," I told Dark Erik. "You're me, my subconscious or whatever. Point is, you know me better than anyone else."

I reached out and grabbed a small seedling attached to a mangrove root. Viscous, dark sap ran in between my fingers.

"This is my power." I put my fingers in my mouth and drank the disgusting black goo.

It was like drinking electricity. My body visibly glowed and I felt like screaming in pure ecstasy.

"And I think it's about time I use it."

Because lives were at stake. Because it was time to grow up. Because no one, not Gil, not Lilith, not the angels, not even God—no one will harm the ones I care about.

Period.

I felt Dark Erik shift again and he placed his hand on my shoulder. I had to accept him. So, I closed the distance and embraced him. My power, my bane—I accepted it all.

Dark Erik's heart glowed until there was a small explosion of light. His body melted into thick, black colored liquid. It spread around my body and settled like a second skin.

It was an extraordinary experience, as if a large weight had been lifted off of my chest. In a few seconds, Dark Erik and real Erik became one and the same. My skin was obsidian colored and red energy emanated from inside me.

The mangroves began shifting. They snaked closer and closer, until they began constricting me. But this wasn't like Lilith's appendage. There was no pain or panic.

The black mangrove roots were an extension of Dark Erik, just a different manifestation of the same power.

I felt power surge throughout my body. It was the strangest feeling. I felt as rested as if I had slept for days but at the same time I felt as if I had been struck by lightning and every cell in my body became a nuclear reactor.

I felt one with my power, finally understanding it.

And in that understanding, I realized there was so much more. The top half of the tree, the part hidden behind very sky itself—that part remained foreign. In fact, it was as if there was a barrier and I could never cross it.

But no matter. I had enough power right here and now. I felt one with the Ashura plane, and felt its pulse synch with my own, as the world and I became one.

And with in my newfound power, I willed myself back to life.

I felt a rush as I transcended dimensions and emerged from Ashura back to Earth.

I was back in my body, still a bloody mess, and felt myself get up. The rush of sensations nearly overwhelmed me and for a long while I was frozen in place as my brain sorted through the barrage of signals it was getting.

A mass of shadows covered my body like a second skin. My healing powers went ballistic and my injuries began healing in seconds. It happened so fast I didn't even feel the pain of my bones and tendons being reconstructed.

I looked at the mirror and saw that I was fully clothed in a red shirt and black pants. My usual working attire. The shroud of shadows parted, revealing my leather trench coat underneath. Darkness trailed all over my body, covering me from head to toe and giving me a really ominous appearance.

I felt a familiar pulse of magic—Djinn. A shadowy tendril wrapped around the sword and brought it to my hand. The blade glowed eagerly.

I felt powerful, but still, I knew I had yet to reach the full potential of these new powers.

I exhaled deeply. My magical senses picked up Lilith's not-so-subtle trail and I bolted after her.

Time to show that goddess the true meaning of power.

Chapter 21

I followed Lilith's trail towards the dance hall only to find a barren room. There was no sign of a fight or supernatural activity.

Nothing, not even so much as a scratch.

And yet, my senses had led me here. I was not mistaken, this was the correct place. My power was enough to batter away any glamour or illusion, so that ruled out that possibility.

I felt something vibrate in my coat and felt around for it. It was a small, outdated cellphone, the kind that looked like a bar of soap, had no camera, and was virtually indestructible.

"Hello?" I said cautiously.

There was a beeping noise.

"Mr. Ashendale?" said a melodic voice on the other end.

"Yeah."

"Welcome back to the land of the living. Please, hold the line."

And just like that the phone beeped again.

"Wait, what the-"

But it was too late. The automated female voice informed me that my call was being transferred and *Stairway to Heaven* began playing. I rolled my eyes. Angels—they should have put 'thou shalt not use obvious clichés' in their stone tablets.

At least it wasn't *Knocking on Heaven's Door*.

After a couple of minutes I heard some static and Amaymon's voice came through.

"Who are you and what the fuck are you doin' in my head?"

I could have hugged him right there and then.

"Amaymon, it's me," I said.

"Erik?" He didn't give me time to answer. "Where the fuck have you been? It's goddamn chaos out here."

"I was sorta dead."

"Them angels popped out and transported Lilith and the rest of us onto a different ship. They got us in a time loop so that we don't affect the rest of the world," he explained.

So, that's what was going on. Damn sneaky angels.

"How do I get there?" I asked.

"I'll open up a portal for you. And haul ass over here 'cause it ain't pretty."

Before I put the phone away I heard him call out.

"Hey, Erik. If you die on me again, I'll come find you in Hell and kick your dumb ass outta there."

I smiled. Amaymon had his own way of caring.

"Got it," I said.

The line went dead and soon after the phone dissolved

into nothing.

I felt Amaymon's portal and followed the signal, which led me outside to the viewing decks. A portal swirled in front of me, three feet from the steel railing. Leave it to Amaymon to open a portal in midair, a hundred feet above sea level. I swung over the railing and held fast. The primal fear of heights that all humans possess sent me into a momentary panic.

But that was human emotion, and whatever was inside of me was definitely not human. I could feel the shadows batting away any concern or fear with an ironclad determination, and one long breath later I was leaping into the swirling mass of color and magic.

The portal spat me out into an empty tanker. It was a miracle this thing was still afloat. The metal was dented and rusty and there were grooves, burns and rips all over the place. Blood covered the floor and I realized I was stepping on human remains. It was a gore-splattered mess.

And in the middle of it all was Lilith.

She was no longer the immaculate beauty that glamoured me. Her body was a mass of scales and spines, constantly shifting. It was as if she had a million different bodies and couldn't decide which one to adopt. So, she mixed and matched different monsters together to create a bizarre, ever-shifting abomination.

She had Abigail in the air, constricting her neck with just one hand, just like she had done with me.

Amaymon bolted towards her and lashed out with his

foot. Lilith caught the blow with her stomach and I heard something crunch. Ribs tore from her torso and splattered against the walls.

But the Sin remained unfazed.

Lilith's body sealed itself together in a disgusting series of squelches. Her free hand was a cross between a paw and a bird's leg. She swatted at Amaymon, batting the demon away from her.

No wonder she messed me up so badly. Amaymon was a powerhouse; to swat him away so casually was no easy feat.

Normally, I wouldn't stand a chance, but now I felt more powerful than the both of them combined.

I could destroy her. I *had to*.

"Hey, bitch!"

My yell made everyone in the room freeze and look in my direction. I must have been quite the scene: a shadow-clad, trench coat wearing figure holding a glowing, blue sword.

Admit it, that's damn cool.

I channeled my power into the sword and slashed. A crescent-shaped energy beam streaked towards Lilith, three times the size of my previous versions. The attack was so fast it actually created a sonic boom and warped the space it passed through. The metal walls around us crunched as the attack shot forwards and into the Sin.

The spell enveloped Lilith and sent her flying. The arm constricting Abigail was torn off. Abigail crouched and retched on the floor as she ripped away the dismembered arm from her neck.

"Get your own succubus," I said, flipping the demoness off.

Lilith emerged, every inch of her skin charred and steam hissing out of her.

"You," she snarled. Her body began repairing itself. "I killed you once already."

I shrugged. "No rest for the wicked. Or maybe it's you who's impotent."

"Ouch. Nice burn," Amaymon said giving me a thumbs-up.

"This time I'll make sure you stay dead," Lilith snarled. Her arm had regenerated into a weird tentacle with hooks at the end. They latched onto me, ensnaring into my flesh with impunity.

I felt pressure around me. Lilith was trying to enter my mind again.

Yeah, right. Like anyone could handle the power I had right then.

I unleashed a burst of power and the shadows soared. Lilith was sent staggering.

"Gonna have to try much harder than that," I said.

"Watch your tongue, boy," she spat. Then she smiled cruelly. "Before I'll rip it off for you."

She reached down and grasped the head of a dead man next to her. He looked like one of the passengers from the cruise ship. Maybe he was accidentally transported with Lilith when the angels did their swapping act. It's not as if those fluffy winged cretins gave a damn about the individual if their death served a higher purpose.

Or maybe they just didn't bother cleaning up the ones that were already dead. Ironically, angels weren't that big on funerary rites.

Lilith ripped the dead guy's head off and reached down into his neck cavity.

I don't want to describe the next two seconds. It's bad enough I had to suffer through that nightmare. Trust me, I'm doing you a favor.

Let's just say there was a lot of crunching, slurping and chewing. And once she was done, only a handful of hollow bones remained, which she just chucked away.

I realized what we were to her: spare parts. That's how she fueled her transformations. She sucked out minerals, chemicals and tissue from her victims and transmuted that into whatever she needed.

Must be how she created demons.

But that power was also Life magic; and no one can use Life magic. No one can just *create* things. It's one of the rules of our universe—we can change energy from one form into another but never create it out of thin air.

And yet, there she was, using magic privy to gods. Was she really a goddess?

A sudden movement snapped me out of my haze.

Lilith appeared a few feet away from me. I took a step backwards and lifted my sword. Her arm shot out and a pair of oversized jaws clamped down on my shoulder. The shadows absorbed the brunt of the damage and I managed to dodge away nearly unscathed.

I flicked Djinn and severed her arm, but Lilith gave no

quarter. She morphed her other arm into a pair of long, curved claws and swung at my face.

Amaymon threw panel of metal between the claws and my eye, and hit Lilith squarely in the face. At the same time, I slashed with an enhanced Djinn and the blast threw Lilith backwards. Her body smashed against the wall, leaving a human shaped dent.

Amaymon appeared to my right. "'Sup?"

"Oh, nothin' much," I replied. "Died, had a life changing revelation, and came back even more awesome than before."

Amaymon raised his eyebrows. "Sounds like a lot of work. Meet anyone down there?"

"Nah. I may have hugged my subconscious, though."

"You're so gay."

Lilith was back up. "How dare you jest in the middle of our confrontation?"

"'Cause you're a joke," Amaymon replied.

We bumped fists and smirked at each other. Lilith let out a shriek of frustration and her body exploded into a different shape. It was as if there was a cage fight going on underneath her skin.

"You got a plan?" whispered my familiar.

"We hit it hard and fast. Your priority is to get the girl out of here. Then come back to help me out."

Amaymon grinned wickedly. "Hard and fast. Just the way I like it."

The demon blurred as he rushed at Lilith. He swiped at her legs, causing her to stumble to one side.

A goat leg shot out and kept her from falling. The Sin spun and a crocodile tail whipped at Amaymon. He jumped above the tail and both his hands smashed into the side of her head. Lilith's ears became ram horns but Amaymon's raw strength was just too great. He clapped her head, crushing those horns and comically flattening her head.

But Lilith wasn't down just yet.

A thick rhino's horn grew from her forehead and she stabbed forwards.

I was at her side and grabbed the horn, pulling her upwards and bringing Djinn down on her neck. I gave a violent twist and heard her neck break. At the same time I drove her to the ground and kicked her side. Djinn's blade elongated to the size of a broadsword and I stabbed downwards.

She rolled away, trailing blood and guts.

I looked around and saw that Amaymon had disappeared together with Abigail.

"Just you and me now, Bridezilla," I snarked at Lilith.

The Sin snarled and lunged for another dead body. But I wasn't just going to let her resupply. I took a step and Lilith fell face forwards. Her fingers morphed into a nest of snakes and I hacked them away but it was too late. She was inches away from the body.

I instinctively reached out with my free hand and grabbed. A shadow hand shot out and grabbed her outstretched arm. I jerked her away from the body and the shadows followed the motion, wrenching Lilith away from the corpse. I sent an energy wave at the poor dead bastard, reducing the body to ash.

"No meal breaks for you," I said.

She snarled in response and raced towards me.

"Surround it!"

Gil's shrill order was accompanied by two bulky rockets of light. The two angels grabbed Lilith savagely. Light and sound exploded like a million flash bang grenades going off at once. The angels began massacring Lilith piece by piece, scorching her with light and fire. Parts of her body began falling off, and were reduced to ash before they hit the ground.

They were winning. The angels were kicking ass in an awesome display of angelic badassery.

"Not like this," she screamed. Darkness rose from Lilith and it began surrounding the angels.

"I will not die at the hands of Heaven's agents," she said. "I am Lilith, Mother of all Demons. Now perish from existence and nourish my children."

Her darkness pulled them close to her and she began *eating* the angels. There was a scream of pure primal ecstasy and she morphed again. A pair of enormous wings spread from behind her. They were angelic in shape but colored an ashen black. Instead of the majestic, pristine wingspan, hers were mangled and misshapen.

The rest of her body resumed a humanoid shape with dark colored scales covering every inch of her skin. Bony spikes and quills jutted out from her as well as her wings.

"Die."

Lilith's quills shot out towards Gil and I as we just stood

there, still in shock that she could just eat up two angels.

Gil's reaction was much quicker than mine.

"No!" she yelled. Her small frame was soon in front of me and I felt her magic take effect.

And I could swear that for the briefest of seconds she was surrounded by white light and smoke.

Her wind spell deflected most of the spikes, but some still made it through. I pushed Gil out of the way and felt two of them pierce my side and leg.

Lilith yelled and turned to face the ceiling. Her wings morphed again and this time claws grew from them. She ripped the roof open, exposing the evening sky above, and with a powerful flap of her wings she escaped through the hole she had just made.

"I'm going after her," Gil said as she ran towards the stairs.

"No, Gil. Wait for me." I took one step and fell down. My leg had gone numb. Those spikes must have had some kind of poison in them.

"I'm not going to let her escape, Erik. You get yourself healed and then come back me up. I'll keep her occupied until then," she replied without stopping. She disappeared soon after and I was left there with a numbing sensation. I gritted my teeth, grabbed the first quill and pulled.

Chapter 22

I cringed against the pain as I wrenched those quills out of my leg. Shadows coagulated around the wounds and soon I was able to walk straight again. My strength soon returned and I chased after Gil.

My sister can be so stubborn at times.

She was the brains and I the brawn—that's been our dynamic ever since we were kids. She wasn't one to lose her cool and chase after her hunt. Whoever pressured her into capturing Lilith must have gotten deep inside her head.

And that was definitely not a good thing.

The door was open and soon I was standing on the large open plain of the metal decks. Just as I made it through the door, I saw Gil's petite figure shoot straight into the wall. There was a sickening crunch as her head smacked against the metal and she crumpled down, unconscious.

Lilith screamed from the other side of the deck.

She was about five feet off the ground and spread out ten feet wide like a grotesque canvas. There was an arm in one place, then a few feet away was her ankle, then her head, and tail and torso and wings were all spread out in different places.

The air around Lilith's limbs swirled and I immediately recognized my sister's space distortion spell. Lilith wasn't directly damaged. The space she occupied was divided into little chunks and jumbled up at random.

In short, the bitch wasn't going anywhere.

I knelt by my sister and felt a tingle of magic. White fog gently emanated from around her. It swirled around my black shadows like a Yin-Yang symbol. The resulting static created a small shock that prickled my skin.

I filed the event away and made a mental note to ask my sister what was going on with her later. But for now, I focused on bringing her back to the real world.

I reached inside her pocket, pulled out an old silk handkerchief and tied it around her head. That stopped the small trickle of blood and I felt her stir.

"Please be gentler with my head," she said groggily. Her hand reached up and she frowned at me.

"You ruined my favorite handkerchief," she said waving it in front of my face.

"You sent a thug after me and had my office demolished," I replied matter-of-factly as I helped her up.

She smiled. "Bill me."

"I intend to."

Lilith screamed again. I felt her power rage against the spell binding her and inch by inch she began to break free. The distorted space began shrinking and shrinking, until she was starting to come together again.

Gil grunted in effort as she grabbed the air in front of her and twisted. The space distortion spell twisted into a shredding vortex. The Sin looked like she was being sucked in a garbage disposal unit.

Only a bit was left.

Just a little more, I thought.

Then Gil suddenly buckled, her energy gone. Lilith was released and she burst into a flock of swirling bats that clustered into each other. And after some flapping, there she stood, hunched over and looking like she'd been run over by a truck.

"She can use Life magic," Gil wheezed. "It's her original power, Erik. Not the Sin's." She managed to sit up. "I need to come up with a plan. Could you keep her occupied and listen at the same time?"

I nodded and spun Djinn around my finger. I'd never tried anything like this before but it was like I already knew the limits of these new powers, even though this was the first time I was using them.

Shadows surrounded the glowing blue sword as it spun using the ring as its axis. My magic increased its speed until the short sword spun so fast that it emitted a faint buzzing noise. I flicked the weapon at Lilith and a tendril of darkness connected the spinning buzz saw that Djinn had become to my hand, giving me complete control over my weapon.

The sword zigzagged through the demon, shredding off entire limbs but flying away before Lilith could swat it and knock it astray. Instead all she could do was stumble, scream, and burn through her biological resources.

"Lilith was originally capable of Life magic," Gil said. "The Sin is just a mantle of power, a boost."

"Meaning?" I kept my focus on Djinn, controlling it through the tendril of darkness.

"Meaning she could create life, but not like this," Gil explained. "This morphing must be the Sin's power. That's what's driving her to feed off people."

"I need a way to kill her, Gil," I responded irritably.

"But something's wrong here," she continued, completely ignoring me. "After the angels damaged her, she can't fully control her transformations."

Her words brought back to mind the visions I had when Lilith was disguising herself as Rose. I remembered being mentally connected to Lilith—the original version, not the Sin of Lust—and her eagerness to show her new powers. Her need to be noticed again, to be recognized and worshipped like the old days.

But the fact that she could still hold onto those feelings meant that the Sin hadn't completely taken hold of her. Which meant…

"She defected from the rest of the Sins," I said. Of course. That right there was a piece of valuable information that had completely escaped me, but now made perfect sense. "Her power is still incomplete."

Gil nodded at me, clearly on the same train of thought. "If that's the case then the Sin itself is no longer under her control and it'll turn on her."

"English, Gil," I said.

"She'll go back to her original self," my sister explained. "A monster-spewing mess. Except this time, they are all still contained inside of her. Push her far enough and she literally won't be able to hold herself together."

"Interesting," I said.

Now, *that* was something I could use.

I willed Djinn back to me and pulled on the tendril. The sword flew back into my waiting hand, and as my fingers wrapped around the hilt the blade exploded in azure light.

"I'm not sure that destroying her would be the best of ideas," Gil said. "I would much rather capture her."

There it was, the Warlock instinct: capture and experiment on.

Until a traitor comes along and releases her again, just like they did with the rest of the Zoo.

No. Hell no. Lilith had to die. Period.

I pointed the sword at the Sin.

"No way, Gil," I said. "She's getting destroyed."

"I don't think-" she began.

"Enough with the thinking," I yelled. "There's the enemy and our job is to take her down before she kills us all."

Gil lowered her eyes.

"You can't contain her," I said a little gentler. "No one can."

My sister may be stubborn but she can see reason. Slowly, she nodded.

"I can manage one more spell," she said. Her expression hardened. Whatever indecision was going on inside her head had been settled and she was back to her ruthless self.

"Any ideas?" I asked.

She smiled. I hadn't seen that smile in quite a while. That devious grin could only mean she was finally ready to play the ace up her sleeve.

"Magnet," she said.

Magnet was a combination spell we used back in the day when we were still kids. It was Gil's invention, a spell designed to capture the enemy in space time barrier. That was just part one.

Part two was me coming in with an attack from the outside. The barrier attracted the offensive spell like a magnet—hence the name—and magnified it tenfold.

The last time we had used this particular combination was when we were still teens, still learning the ropes of magic. There was very little power behind our magic back then, barely enough to take down mid-sized monsters.

Now, with both Djinn and my shadows, I shuddered to think what ten times my regular power could generate.

Ah, well. I guess there's only one way to find out.

I nodded at Gil and returned her grin. Let's see Lilith walk out of this one.

Chapter 23

When Gil said she could do one more spell, she meant she *could* cast her magic but would faint immediately afterwards.

I should have known. My sister and I were both stubborn and headstrong.

I could see sweat glistening on her face as she summoned the very last reserves of her power.

There was no motion, no yell or chant or magic word. My sister's power was in her mind. She knew every spell and counter spell in the books and exactly when to use them. Her brain could spin circles around Einstein's and leave him wanting more.

Only problem was that she lacked the raw power to perform most of those spells. So, instead of crushing the enemy like I do, she used magic in such a way so as to rely on her concentration rather than brute force.

The air around Lilith distorted. Her limbs were pressed into her main body. It was like she had the most powerful magnet on her chest and everything was being driven inside.

She struggled and thrashed wildly. Anything that grew from her body, Gil immediately crushed back down. And for a while it seemed like my sister was winning.

But she was only human and the spell took extraordinary concentration on her part. She had to immediately analyze whatever grew out of Lilith and apply the correct amount of pressure on it without sacrificing power from other areas. She had a mind like a computer, able to do three high concentration things at once.

Meanwhile, I quit playing Solitaire on my computer when the cards move too fast.

She gave one final push and I actually heard Lilith's internal organs rupture.

Remind me never to mess with my sister—she can literally fuck you up with her mind.

Gil fell down, completely spent. Shadow tendrils reached out from my body and gently caught her, easing her onto the ground. She had done her part and now it was my turn.

But first I had to make sure she was safe.

I knelt down and pulled her sleeve up. There, on her forearm, was an intricate tattoo: a summoning sigil. I reached behind her ear, where a small cut was oozing droplets of blood, and smeared some blood on the tattoo.

I felt the air shift and Mephisto emerged. He took one look at Lilith and then at me, and a glare appeared on his face.

"Where the hell were you?" I growled. If he had been there for my sister like he was supposed to be, then she might not have had to push herself so much. Not even my familiar, despite all of his crap, would just abandon me. Gil could have died, just because this guy didn't do his freaking job.

Mephisto's thin eyebrows arched up. "That is between me and Master Gil," he shot back curtly.

You know how some guys make you want to hit them repeatedly? This guy was one of them. But I didn't have time to fool around. Gil had to be far away from here before I finished off Lilith.

"Take your master and leave here," I ordered.

He remained standing there, with his arms folded.

"Master Erik." He spat my name out like a bad taste. "I do not take orders from you."

There was a burning sensation in my stomach, like someone poured acid down there. At the same time, I felt Lilith's struggling. Gil's magic was only temporary and the Sin was breaking it down.

I had to act fast, and the last thing I needed was this guy's bullshit.

You remember when I said stress, fear and anger can kick your magic up a notch? Well, I was bathing in those feelings and it now started to show.

I felt my shadows flare and something deep inside me clicked. All that untapped potential was released and my entire body tingled. Bones cracked as they shifted. I didn't see the magic penetrate and enhance every bone, muscle and fibre of my body but I felt it.

I straightened myself and was suddenly head to head with Mephisto's six feet.

I cast one look down at my own body. My clothes

dissolved and it was like someone had drenched me in black paint. I was covered in darkness from head to toe and became a physical manifestation of my hidden powers.

I had become Dark Erik.

Every bone ached. My fingers lengthened, bones breaking past the skin and hardening into claws. The same thing happened to my elbows, shoulders, knees and ankles. Bone grew past the skin and formed small bumps and spikes around the joints. I reached behind me and felt each one of my vertebrae protruding.

Something pressed against my lips. I prodded around my mouth with my tongue and felt a row of sharp fangs in place of my usual teeth.

I caught a glance of myself on a polished piece of metal. The color of my eyes caught my attention; my red eyes.

Darkness flared around me like a robe and as I exhaled, steam came out of my mouth.

And best of all, Mephisto recoiled backwards in terror.

"Dog!" I snapped. My voice had become more glottal and feral. I pointed one clawed finger at him. "I am Erik Ashendale, heir to the Ashendale Power and Title. I am a descendant of the first Warlocks."

I had never uttered that before. I guess that was my subconscious finally vocalizing when I always wanted to say to this jackass. Maybe this was me finally accepting who I was and saying it out loud was a way of setting it in stone.

I glared at the demon and smirked. I raised my fist and heard knuckles cracking.

"Don't fuck with me," I said.

Then, Mephisto did the one thing I least expected him to do: he bowed.

"As you wish," he replied. The look on his face suggested he might hurl at any moment.

The demon scooped up my sister and stood in front of a portal. Before he stepped through, he turned around. "Congratulations on discovering your roots, Master Erik," he muttered.

There we go again with the cryptic crap.

"Is there something you want to say?" I snapped.

"Nothing you will not understand with a little self-discovery," he said.

I did not like the look in his eyes. He always wore that look when he taught us magic as kids—like he knew something we didn't. Like he was just wanted to toy with us, waiting for just the right time to screw us over.

Before I could say anything else, he disappeared. Which was probably a good thing, since Lilith was about to break free.

"You!" she screamed, clawing at me with something that resembled a mangled hand. "I recognize that power. You and him are the same. Did he give you his power?"

Was everyone here aware of what was going on except me? "What the hell are you talking about, you crazy bitch?"

"He. The one that matters, the only one that ever mattered. The first and last," she raved, maniacally jerking her head about. "No, no it can't be. It's a similar power but not the same. But you and I are the same, Warlock. We have the power to shape the world as we see fit. Join me, Warlock."

Seriously? After all she did she expected me to just team up with her? She must really be cracked.

"Don't you wanna see my resume first?" I replied as I picked up Djinn. The blade glowed intensely as shadows encased it.

"What?" She was just about to break free. "Speak clearly, Warlock. Will you join me?"

I let out a bark of laughter. Djinn's blade engorged disproportionately and the tip embedded itself in the metallic deck. The azure energy blade had widened to about my width.

Even if I were evil, I doubt I'd join her. I mean, she doesn't get any of my jokes—it just wouldn't work out in the end.

"First off, I am not *Warlock*," I replied. "The name is Erik."

My body shifted into a battle stance and held Djinn's blade at my side, ready for a strike.

"And as for your offer," I growled, "here's my answer."

My magic flared and I poured it all into the sword. Layer upon layer of energy and shadows piled around the blade until it was twice my size, and still growing. Shadows and dark red pigmentation mixed with the raging blue light of the sword. The metal of the deck sizzled and paint evaporated.

And I still kept pouring in more magic.

Djinn could take all of that power. This sword was a family heirloom from my deceased mother's side. It was thousands of years old and made of magic that was long lost.

But now it was *my* channel, and was as much a part of me as my magic.

My new powers extended to the area around me, affecting not just space but also time. I saw Lilith's mouth stop mid-sentence. She was probably going to spout more bullshit.

The waves halted mid-crash as if someone had hit the pause button on the universe and it froze.

All except me.

I kept charging Djinn until it reached a critical point. That's when I heard myself exhale and time flowed normally again. Lilith said something but I couldn't hear her over the loud pitch of Djinn and all that power inside of it.

Lilith was floating a few feet off the deck and was seconds away from liberating herself.

That was enough time—I swung with all my might.

"FUCK YOU!" I yelled, releasing all of that pent up energy.

I brought the gargantuan sword around in a horizontal slash. Metal crunched beneath my feet from the pressure. Even the waves below were pushed backwards, rocking the entire ship to one side.

Djinn's energy blade shot out, rocketing towards Lilith's screaming figure. My magic was stronger than I thought. The energy was so intense it was distorting space and time along its trajectory.

The already immense energy met Gil's Magnet spell and multiplied. The resulting energy mass carried Lilith upwards and exploded violently. I was sent reeling backwards from the recoil of the spell, and the ship threatened to capsize.

At the point of impact, a small vortex appeared and sucked everything in. A pillar of water rose up and exploded in a shower of rain. I stabbed my sword into the metal and held fast against the rocking ship. Another aftershock followed soon and created another explosion, leaving me momentarily blind and deafened.

And then, suddenly, it was all over.

The ship settled down, rocking gently. The waves were still upset and seawater rained down.

The attack had distorted space and time on a massive scale. The sun began to peak—I must have sent us at least five hours forward in time.

On the far horizon I saw the cruise ship, with its passengers still unaware of how close they came to being Lilith's personal buffet, and I exhaled in relief. It was always a good day when you prevented a massacre.

My magical senses confirmed that Lilith—or Lust—had gone, with no trace of their presence left behind. All that was left was a blob of slime—ectoplasm, left in the wake of one of the most terrifying creatures to ever cross over to our plane.

I gazed at the rising sun, the first peaks of daybreak, and laughed giddily.

This was it. All that pain and suffering was over now. I had finally killed the Sin of Lust and now the world could breathe a sigh of relief.

It was finally over… or so I thought.

Chapter 24

I felt familiar magic behind me and turned around. Standing—or rather, hovering—on the ship's deck was an astral projection of my sister. She looked exactly like a ghost, with an opaque form but otherwise behaved exactly like a normal human being.

She called out to me. "Erik."

"Gil, are you okay?" I asked.

The apparition appeared tired but my sister nodded nonetheless. "Mephisto took me back to the pier. Was that you who shifted time?"

"Yeah. Didn't mean to." I looked at my hands. They were still covered in shadows and underneath the swirling black I could still feel the sharpness of my claws and the power coursing within me.

"What the hell is going on?" I asked.

"I don't know. But we can figure it out later," she said. "For now, just keep calm and relax. It should dissipate naturally."

"Good, 'cause I'd hate to answer the door like this," I replied sarcastically.

"I'd call it an improvement over your usual get up," came Amaymon's voice. The demon leapt from the ship's funnel structure and landed heavily next to me.

Then he sized me up. "You look different," he said. "Did you do something with your hair?"

I heard myself laugh in a throaty, glottal voice that wasn't really mine.

"Glad to see you too. Where'd you drop Abigail?" I asked him.

"With her," he replied, pointing at the astral projection.

"Please, don't touch me," Gil replied. "I don't have the strength to reform myself around physical objects."

"That ain't the reason chicks don't let me touch them."

"Why did you leave Abigail with her?" I asked.

"Hey, I got jumped by angels," he replied defensively. "And as much as I don't like them, those clowns won't do anything rash. Besides, the girl is a liability on the battlefield."

I glared at Gil.

"We have no use for her, Erik," she replied placidly. "We'll keep her safe here. Mephisto is cloaking the entire area. You remember how good he is at hiding stuff."

Yeah, I did. I shook my head, repressing that particular memory from my childhood. Sooner or later I was going to have to sit down and deal with all of that stuff.

I chose later.

"Fine," I said, waving a clawed hand at her. "But if you

let anything happen to her, I'm holding you responsible. Am I clear?"

"Careful, brother," she said in icy tones. "One might mistake your new appearance for a demon."

It doesn't take a genius to decipher the threat underneath. Guess she wasn't above hunting family.

"Bring it on, Gil," I replied. "I took your forces down once and I can do it again."

"Remind me again why you guys don't got a sitcom on TV?" Amaymon said.

My sister and I glared at each other one last time.

"Just keep her safe, okay?" I finally said.

"Fine. And you clean up after your mess, brother," she replied.

"What mess?"

She pointed behind me. "That one."

I thought it was ectoplasm. I mean it looked like ectoplasm, felt like ectoplasm and behaved like ectoplasm.

Only ectoplasm doesn't usually stick to ships like tar and converge in a disgusting, writhing puddle, like an enormous piece of jello. In the middle of the ectoplasmic mass I could distinctly see a face—Lilith's face.

"No," she moaned. "No, my children, no."

But whatever was inside of her tore her open and Lilith exploded into a million pieces. Then, like a terrible B-movie, each of those pieces grew larger, and larger, taking on a new shape. Soon the deck was filled with every demon, monster and nightmare imaginable.

They came in all shapes and sizes: giant spiders with fangs

on their faces, chiropteran demons flapping around like oversized bats, three-legged crows the size of an apartment block and canines of all sorts. Some even resembled werewolves, the Hollywood kind.

But worst of all were the asmodaii. They were humanoid with abnormally thin and slender bodies, ranging between five and seven feet tall. They walked on two legs—and that was pretty much all they had in common with us. Their legs were reverse jointed, like a dog's, and their crooked arms ended in either claws or spikes or blades of sorts. Their leathery hides were dark grey in color, like exhaust fumes.

Worst of all, the asmodaii had no faces; just heads with patches of black where a face should be. But they did have wide mouths, lined with rows of jagged teeth like a shark's.

These were the foot soldiers of Hell: killing machines bred only for death and destruction.

"It seems that your attack caused her to lose her ability to hold herself together," Gil said from behind me. "Now, every creature she can compose out of her remains will emerge." Then she gave me her 'I told you so' look. "I suspected this would happen. That's why you should have-"

Amaymon swiped at the projection, scattering it. "I hate nags," he said with a shrug.

I couldn't have agreed more.

One of the monsters, a half-human half-serpent, thrashed about and flung the remaining chunks of Lilith's ectoplasm into the ocean. Not that I was complaining. There was a veritable horde on the ship now, more than enough for us to deal with. Maybe the running water would dissolve the rest of the ectoplasm.

See? I can be optimistic.

"What a merry bunch of monsters we have here." Mephisto's cold voice signaled his arrival and he landed gently beside me on the deck. "Master Gil sent me for backup," he explained.

"You sure you don't wanna sit this one out, bro?" Amaymon hollered. "You ain't exactly the front line fighting type. And bitching behind their backs ain't gonna be much help."

Mephisto snorted and offered his brother a condescending smile. "Sticks and stones may break my bones-"

Amaymon ripped apart a sheet of metal and twisted it into a pipe, like a rolled up magazine. "You wanna test that theory?" he said sadistically.

I slipped in between them and held my arms apart. "Hey, guys, we're surrounded by demons. Take your issues out on them."

There was a brief second where we all stood still. The only sounds were the crashing of waves against the sides of the ship, punctuated by the scratching of claws against the metal of the decks.

They were sizing us up: two ancient demons and a wizard with mysterious powers.

Three idiots facing an army of monsters numbering over fifty. I could see their muscles tensing and relaxing, ready to pounce on us. And if they did, it was sure to be a massacre.

One of the asmodaii took a cautious step forwards and

my power reacted. It wasn't my intention—the shadows seemed to have a mind of their own.

A shadow tendril shot forwards and impaled the asmodaii. More tendrils branched out from the main one, shredding the monster. Then, just as quickly, the shadows retracted back into my body and there was silence once more.

But the damage had been done, and less than a second later, war erupted.

Chapter 25

We rushed at the horde.

Amaymon leapt high above the majority of the monsters, landing in their midst. That way he could take them out from the center. Mephisto took to the skies, felling aerial monsters in his wake. Their attacks, and the ship's construction, pushed the rest of the monsters in one direction—towards me.

My body moved on its own and I found myself lunging forwards. Werewolves, naga, gremlin-looking creatures, chiropterans: they all fell to my blade as I unleashed onslaught after onslaught. I relished in the rawness of the killing, the spilling of blood and ectoplasm. The shadows reacted faster than my blade or body, impaling and crushing all those that slipped beyond my human senses.

The rawness, the purity, and the need for destruction, they were all so addictive. I knew this was Dark Erik talking and that these were unfiltered emotions. But I wanted to let them run wild. I wanted to cut loose.

The other side of me, the side tempered by control and helping others, now began fighting back. Now there was a tug of war between nature and civilization. Slowly but surely I was regaining control over my emotions, but I couldn't have picked a worse place. Direct battle is not where you play mind games. One false move and your head could be rolling.

And with these guys, that was literal.

There was a group of asmodaii a few feet away that incurred my wrath. One thing you learnt rather quickly was who were pawns and who were the leaders. These asmodaii, despite their legendary fighting prowess, stood back watching.

Waiting.

I willed my shadow forwards. A wave of black thinned and elongated from my left arm and passed through the first two. I'm sure if they had a face they would look puzzled as to why their bodies had separated in two. For the remaining three, I clawed with my real hand and the shadows imitated. A giant hand of black grabbed the asmodaii and crushed them together. I kept pressing and pressing until I made demon soup in my big, black fist. Once the job was done the shadows retracted.

Mission accomplished, achievement unlocked.

I heard a sickening crack behind me as Amaymon grabbed something reptilian and tore it apart as if it were a sheet of paper.

A large tarantula had made it up the funnel and was about to jump on Mephisto, who floated in mid-air like a paper kite. Calmly, he spun in midair and spread his arms. A violent wind surrounded the spider.

The demon closed his eyes and began tapping his fingers like a piano player. The wind whistled loudly as it scythed through the spider, shredding it. As bits of arachnid and gore rained, he splayed his arms and bowed deeply.

"Show off," Amaymon said, suddenly appearing beside me. At the same time he pulled a naga by the tail, ripping her in half. Then, he calmly dismembered her head and kicked it like a football. The projectile thwacked against Mephisto, who flipped his brother off.

"You know," he said. "This all seems just a bit too easy. I thought Lilith was supposed to spew out the best of the best."

"I concur, brother," came Mephisto's voice. "These are no Alphas."

"Isn't that a good thing?" I asked.

"If we were mistaken, yes," he replied. "But not if there is something else in store."

"Ah, whatever," interrupted my familiar. "Bring it on, we'll kick their- Erik, watch out!"

I spun and raised my sword.

A pair of fangs descended on me and I barely managed to intercept them with my sword. The giant spider spewed putrid breath and saliva on me as it pressed forwards. I was nearly driven to my knees.

I willed more power in my body and pushed the creature backwards. Once it reared back, I swiped horizontally. Djinn's blade elongated to ten times its length, slicing through all of the spider's legs before retracting back.

The spider crashed down next to me with its ugly head still snapping. I smashed my fist on it and wrapped my arm in a headlock. With a grunt of effort, I ripped the spider's head off, spraying myself with blood and black ichor in the process.

Amaymon let out a low whistle.

Oh, crap. If I can impress that demon with displays of violence, then it was time to check myself.

Before anyone could comment, we all felt something in the atmosphere. From in front of the ship, the air shimmered and light particles, like snowflakes, began dispersing all over the area.

I let the spider's head drop and reached out to grab a particle. It was neither a snowflake nor solid light. It was a small pocket of air and magic which dissolved immediately against my touch. More clustered in front of the ship, like a giant wall.

"Anima particles," Amaymon said.

Anima particles were basically left over magic, tiny amounts of energy that were wasted when a spell was cast. Usually the amount was so small that you couldn't even see them, like dust particles in the wind.

But right over there, there was a solid wall of the damn things. A cluster of anima particles usually meant a summoning ritual of sorts. That kind of magic tended to need so much energy that it left clumps of residue behind. I shuddered as I did some calculations. Whatever monster was coming our way had to be extraordinary powerful to need so much energy that it leaves behind that much residue.

Amaymon's fist shot three inches from my face. An asmodaii fell dead next to me.

"Small fry, first," he said.

And he was right. We could deal with whatever was being summoned later. Right now, I had to deal with the rest of this horde.

Amaymon disappeared again, leaving me to deal with a small squad of asmodaii. I reached down and a shadow hand grabbed the spider's head. I threw it at them.

The lead demon swatted the missile away, but fell to my trick. I was right behind the projectile and stabbed Djinn into his head. I wrenched the blade free with a burst of azure light.

My frenzy felled two more demons before the others dodged away.

They launched an attack, and I countered, killing three more in the process.

I slashed at another one and he evaded perfectly. At the same time, his companion came from the side, complementing his attack. I barely managed to keep up but made it through in one piece.

It occurred to me that the asmodaii had a hive mind, each learning from the rest. That would explain why these two suddenly became so good at keeping up with me. That was why they were the foot soldiers of Hell. They adapted to any situation in a matter of minutes. That was what made them the perfect killing machines.

I blocked a swipe from one at my left and shot a fist of

shadows at the second one, catching him off guard. Asmodaii number two was sent flying off the railing and into the water.

The third demon cocked his head and rushed at me. He feinted and I fell for it. His foot snapped at my knee, sending me crashing down. The asmodaii stabbed forwards with its claws. I swiped with my sword, severing his arm. My own clawed hand raked at his flesh, also tearing off a good chunk of his torso.

The demon fell dead.

But it wasn't over yet. Another asmodaii approached. This one had an inward curving blade in place of its right forearm, and it brought the falx-like weapon down on me. I blocked with Djinn and struggled.

Then, I learned something about my new power: it was temporary. It made you think you were invincible, that you were all powerful, but there was always a catch with that kind of power. It was fading when I needed it the most.

I had made the same mistake as Lilith when she faced me; thinking I was beyond these low-level demons and could easily take them.

Now that I had used my new powers indiscriminately without knowing its limits, I was about to pay a hefty price.

My strength faltered under the blade lock. The asmodaii cocked its head curiously, trying to understand what was going on. I felt weak and tired, and it was showing.

And if there's one thing a super soldier knows how to do, it's exploiting weaknesses.

The asmodaii released the blade lock and leapt high,

landing behind me. I felt a sharp pain in my back followed by a wave of cold. I looked downwards and saw the tip of the demon's weapon jutting from my chest.

Chapter 26

It was like someone had switched off my body but left my brain on.

I was still aware of what was going on. I got stabbed, was probably going to die *again* and there was nothing I could do about it. It wasn't painful. At least not until the asmodaii pulled its blade out and circled in front of me.

I felt my body constricting as my lungs began shutting down. Wave after wave of cold washed over me as blood soaked the decks.

I heard Amaymon scream my name. A pack of lycanthropes ganged up on him as he was momentarily distracted. He went wild, throwing and killing monsters like a berserker.

But it was too late. The asmodaii's other arm was equipped with a pair of curved, dagger-like claws. It raised its hand, ready to strike at my face. It would all be over soon. One of those claws would enter my eye socket and rip my face off. He'd most likely take off a chunk of my brain, too.

I would die instantly, without much pain.

Helpless, I closed my eyes and prepared for the end. I murmured an apology to everyone and found myself thinking 'fuck it all'.

How befitting of me. Maybe they could chisel that on my tombstone.

But once again, the universe wanted to prove me wrong. It was just dumb luck that it actually worked in my favor this time.

Turns out it wasn't my time yet, because right before the asmodaii could shish kebab me, a sword of light sliced through it. The demon exploded in a shower of light.

My savior was literally an angel. It was a glowing humanoid figure clad in armor. And not the modern Kevlar kind either. This guy was in full medieval armor, like he had just stepped out from a Knights of the Round Table reenactment.

Its face was a sculptor's wet dream. You couldn't tell if it belonged to a male or female, only that it was very pretty. A pair of pointy, elf-like ears held back long, flowing, golden hair which shone brighter than the sun.

The whole figure was clad in a halo of pure white light, as if it had its own personal spotlight. The light wavered and I realized those were its wings. Unlike the wings on Gil's angels, this one had a wingspan that was nearly ten meters wide and the wings were made from pure light. It was hard just trying to look at them.

The angel sheathed its sword and the wings wrapped around its body, before shrinking down, and it stopped burning out every retina in a five mile radius.

The newcomer held up the palm of its hand.

Anima particles rushed into it, forming an ever-growing ball of light. The angel's gaze shifted towards me and it thrust the particles into my chest wound.

I felt myself on fire. I heard a roar shake the entire ship and I realized it was me. The shadow rose and covered the height of the ship, destroying demons and monsters at random.

The angel kept shoving anima particles into me as I lay there with my power going out of control. Of course, from a distance, it must have looked like the angel was torturing me. Which explained why Amaymon's fist crashed into the angel and sent it flying.

"The fuck you doing?" he roared.

From the sky, angels descended like blazing meteorites. They were all in full armor, hacking through demons with swords and shields. Four of them landed around Amaymon, who stepped over me protectively.

"Enough!"

The angels scattered as their leader—the one who was shoving anima particles inside me—walked up to us without so much as a scratch. Its wings flared once more and I felt an ocean of power emanating from it.

Oh, crap. This was the Virtue, I realized. This was the guy that was supposed to counter the sin of Lust, an archangel from Heaven itself.

Well, you're too late now, buddy.

"How do you feel, wizard?" he said. I suppose I could call

it a guy; he sounded manly enough. His appearance, on the other hand, made me question my sexuality.

I immediately stopped convulsing and twitching. My shadows retracted and I felt more powerful than I had in years.

"I feel great," I said. I tried extending the shadows consciously and my power responded.

All systems were back online.

"I don't know what you did, but thanks," I said.

Amaymon pointed a finger at him. "Who are you?"

The archangel's melodic voice emanated. "I am Jehudiel, Virtue and Archangel of Heaven." He smiled at me. It was a smile devoid of any real emotion, but hey, at least the guy was trying.

"You are very welcome, Erik Ashendale," he said. "The basis of your power is Life magic, the same kind found in anima particles. It is only natural that you would be compatible."

What?

Me, have Life magic?

Then, I remembered Lilith's final words, when she said we were alike.

Did that mean that I was some sort of god? I waved the thought away. Gods tended to have better lives than mine and not have to worry about taxes or annoying neighbors. If I were a god I wouldn't have had such a hard time in the past three days.

The angel must have read my thoughts. "You will come to understand your power soon, Erik Ashendale," he said. The way he smiled made me think he knew something that he wasn't telling me. Something I should know.

"This is your legacy," he added. "You are the root of it all."

There it was again, the word 'root'. Mephisto had used that, too. What the hell did it mean?

And why does everyone insist on being so damn cryptic?

Jehudiel put his helmet on. "It's time," he said.

I followed his gaze towards the mass of anima particles. I could feel the massive scale of the creature even before it crossed into our plane.

"Dude, you should see your face right now," Amaymon whispered.

I ignored him. Instead, I turned to the angel and asked, "What is that?"

"An Alpha. One of the original demons. Lilith's spawn," he replied. "You must have damaged her too much for her to create just one."

Ah hah! Point for Erik. Suck on that, demon lady.

Jehudiel's wings flared. "That abomination contains what remains of the sin of Lust. It must not be allowed on this plane," he said. "Only once we destroy it will order be restored to this dimension."

Amaymon snorted. "Angels. Always with the order."

At that precise moment the particles parted and revealed a monstrous nightmare.

"Holy crap," I muttered.

"Hey, we got an angel in the house," Amaymon mocked.

"Do not mention the Lord's name in vain," Jehudiel berated.

I did not have a comeback. I was too stunned looking at

the Alpha as it emerged.

The Alpha was larger than the ship we were on. Its torso was a solid barrel of muscle with thick, slimy skin like a squid's. It had a pair of humanoid arms, each knotted with thick muscles. Each finger ended in a thick, black hoof. Its head was a grey blob with a pair of pitch-black, saucer-like eyes. Dagger-like teeth jutted from its mouth. Finally, a pair of bull horns emerged from either side of its head.

The Alpha's lower half was just a set of eight tentacles, each as thick as a telephone pole. Just one slap of those things and the ship would capsize. Its suckers had rows of teeth in them, which could probably rip off the metal sheets of the tanker.

I remembered seeing something like this once in a painting. It was the monster from Shinto mythology: an Ushi-Oni. Think of it as the love child between a Kraken and a Minotaur and you wouldn't be too far off. Even by mythological standards, this was one ugly dude.

Jehudiel gently laid his hand on my shoulder. His touch was electric and warm.

"You and the two demons must keep it occupied," he said, "while my legion and I eliminate the hell-spawn."

"Why don't we trade places?" I shot back. But the archangel had already vanished.

Amaymon slapped my shoulder playfully.

"Looks like it's just you and me against Big Ugly over there," he said. "You got any bright ideas?"

I shrugged. "Not a clue. You?"

"Same."

I groaned. "We are so fucked."

Chapter 27

Keep it occupied he says.

Easy for Jehudiel to say. He's an angel. He's got wings and armor and his own personal laser light show. Not to mention friends. Angel friends, with shiny broadswords and nigh infinite cosmic powers.

All I had was a short sword that was looking more impotent by the second, and a familiar who was probably more curious to see how the Ushi-Oni would flatten me.

The sky darkened as a giant tentacle loomed closer and closer.

Amaymon had already disappeared. I felt my leg muscles scream in protest as I threw myself sideways. The giant limb whipped inches from my face and the ship let out a dying groan and metal screamed. There was a deep dent on the deck. I wondered how many more of those the ship could take. Three, maybe four more hits like that, and we were looking at the ending of *Titanic*.

A second tentacle loomed over and I sprang into action.

No point in trying to stop something so heavy. I would be wasting too much energy. Instead, a shadowy mass shot straight for the tentacle, deflecting it into the water. The splash made the ship lurch violently to one side.

Amaymon tore a chunk of metal from the ship and hurled it at the Ushi-Oni's head. It caught one of the horns and snapped it off.

Meanwhile, wind gathered violently around the beast. Mephisto hovered above the Ushi-Oni like a phantom. His arms were spread eagle and he strained to contain the beast. The wind was so powerful it shredded the beast's rubbery skin. Black ichor oozed from the monster's gaping wounds.

Two of its tentacles fell off and completely shriveled up.

"Amaymon, pin it," I yelled.

The demon gave me the thumbs up and clawed at the air. He lifted upwards and I could hear his yell despite Mephisto's wind.

"Rock the house, baby!"

There was a shudder like a violent earthquake. Whatever Amaymon was doing, it was affecting the whole seabed. Then, giant spikes of stone jutted from the water like icebergs and impaled the Alpha. I shuddered to think of the damage he caused to the planet's tectonic plates in just that one instant.

But this was priority. I could worry about the planet after the giant spawn from another dimension was vanquished.

I stood at the very end of the ship's bow and extended my shadows into the water.

I knew for a fact that I could use magic freely again, that

I didn't need Djinn or channels. My shadows represented my intention and my magic. They were me, and whatever they touched became a part of me and my magic.

I know, it was confusing to me as well. But at that moment it felt as natural as breathing.

My magic extended to the water. I willed it upwards, transmuting it into a solid state. The water spray morphed into a series of thick icicles that shot at the Ushi-Oni from every direction. It worked. The beast screamed as torrents of ink-black blood gushed out from it.

Our assault ended when Mephisto landed on the deck with a thump and was actually wheezing on all fours. Suddenly my body felt as if I had just run a marathon and swam for my life after being chased by dinosaur sharks. I realized that I was back to my old self: no more black skin, or claws, or shadows.

I was back to a human being and had absolutely no advantage in this situation.

The beast groaned as our spells vanished. The rocks were sucked back into the seabed, the wind had vanished into literal thin air and my ice evaporated before you could say 'global warming'.

I saw light around the Ushi-Oni as a legion of angels descended upon it and subdued the beast.

"Wonderful job," Jehudiel said as the archangel helped me up. His touch instantly made me feel better, stronger.

But there were no anima particles I could absorb. Whatever powers I had before had now completely receded back into my subconscious, far from my grasp, and I was left alone with a short sword and a battered body.

"Do not worry," the angel said gently. "You have weakened it sufficiently. One more spell and our mission will be over."

He reached inside his armor and extracted my modified flintlock gun. "I borrowed this in order to prepare our magic."

I snatched the gun away and checked the clip. Empty. What good was a gun without any bullets?

"Heaven entrusts you with its magic," Jehudiel said. He grasped my hand and light emanated from our grip. I felt something small and solid being pressed into my palm, and opened my hand to see what it was.

A bullet.

I stared at it. There was power in the thing, ancient power.

"So, I'm supposed to Rip Van Winkle the bad guy with this?" I asked.

The archangel cocked its head.

That's it. If Heaven doesn't have a sense of humor, I'm booking my ticket for down south.

"It's a bullet, you moron," Amaymon yelled. "Just shoot it before the giant monster flattens us."

Amaymon: resolving self-esteem issues since whenever he was spawned.

Jehudiel smiled. Oh, *that* joke he got.

Douche-bag.

"Have a little faith," he said.

I raised my gun. "I'm not that good with faith. That's

why I carry a gun."

Jehudiel's expression remained unchanged.

"Okay, then," I said. "Let's try it your way."

Despite its weird shape, the bullet fit perfectly inside my firearm.

I aimed the gun at the Ushi-Oni but something stopped me. It was like I was getting instructions downloaded directly into my brain. This wasn't a human bullet; you don't just point and click and expect the thing to die. This was Heaven's magic, a spell created by Jehudiel himself. This thing was designed to destroy every trace of the Sin of Lust and completely eradicate Lilith from the world.

It was magic designed to destroy and repair at the same time. Definitely not a human concept. This was power that no human could conceive, much less create.

I immediately understood what I had to do.

It was like we were all connected telepathically. As soon as I was ready to shoot, the angel soldiers disappeared from around the Alpha and lined up behind Jehudiel. They had no emotions, at least not human ones, but I could sense some curiosity emanating from them. Here was a human doing Heaven's will. One screw up and we're all monster chow.

No pressure, Erik.

I pointed the gun upwards and pushed all my magic into it. This was not just an angelic matter anymore. This spell melded human and angel magic for the purpose of eradicating evil. It all sounded very *Power Rangers* for a moment, but I really didn't mind. For once, I let go of all my cynicism and just accepted the fact that I was doing the right thing, for the right reasons.

And everything else can just get bent.

I pulled the trigger. The recoil was a giant explosion that jarred my entire body and dented the metal floor of the deck beneath my feet.

The bullet itself was a mass of light that rocketed into the sky. We all followed its trajectory, even the Ushi-Oni. It reached the clouds and expanded, tracing light all over the sky.

I felt the connection with the entire sky. I looked down and saw a string of black going from my body all the way into the sky. I was now in control of this Armageddon-level spell. I had willed it to life and now I gave it purpose.

The sky swirled and grey clouds condensed into a swirling mass. Thunder and lightning resounded all over the place. I dropped my gun and focused entirely on the spell, causing black shadows to coalesce inside my right hand as I squeezed it into a fist.

The clouds above clashed together and took on the shape of a giant fist—a giant, titanic imitation of my hand. I flexed a finger and the cloud fist mirrored the movement.

Jehudiel smiled. "The Hand of God," he commented.

Turns out Heaven had a sense of humor after all.

I pulled my fist back and thunder clapped louder than ever with every inch the cloud fist moved. I began feeling giddy with sheer power and felt a painful grin stretch on my lips.

"Harry Potter can kiss. My. Ass!" I yelled in ecstasy.

I punched forwards, towards the Ushi-Oni, with every intention of erasing its presence—and that of Lilith—from the universe.

The gargantuan fist shot forwards, descending on the giant demonic creature. As it fell, the clouds swirled and morphed into a giant spinning lance. The weapon, made out of grey clouds, flashing lightning and roaring thunder, crashed into the Alpha and implied it.

I felt the absolute nature of the magic inside the spell take effect. There was no cry of pain or anger. The Ushi-Oni was summarily shredded on a subatomic level until less than a second later it was destroyed once and for all, leaving behind only silence and a disturbing memory.

The battle was over. I was certain of that now. No more Sin, no more Lilith, no more end of the world.

For now.

All that remained was a whole bunch of questions.

Ah, screw it. I'll save the questions for later. Right now, I needed some sleep. Maybe I should take the week off. God knows I deserve it—and in this case that can very well be literal.

The angels began disappearing one by one.

"Our task is done," Jehudiel said. "I thank you for your cooperation, Erik Ashendale."

I nodded. It wasn't over, not by a long shot.

There will be repercussions for Lilith's death. The whole balance of power had shifted, leaving a void in the universe. I knew Jehudiel wasn't telling me everything, just as I knew he was hiding an ace up his sleeve.

Freaking angels and their mind games. No wonder they get along so well with my sister.

Mephisto came up to me. "Master Erik," he said. "I have orders to escort you to the pier. There, you will meet with Master Gil."

"What about the girl, Abigail?" I asked.

"She has been delivered to your office address and is presently waiting for you there," the demon replied.

His form shimmered and a black dog took his place. "Please, follow me," he instructed as a portal swirled open in front of him.

I groaned. The last thing I wanted was a conversation with my estranged sister. But I suppose that was to be expected, since she was involved in this after all. Not just with the mission but also with the mysterious powers I had gotten. I was sure it had something to do with the family curse and if there was one person who could get to the bottom of that mystery, it was Gil.

"Fine," I said. "But I ain't getting in there."

The dog cocked its head.

"He gets sick from portals. Dude's got a very delicate constitution," Amaymon whispered loudly enough for everyone to hear.

Mephisto let out a short bark. "Then, how do you suppose we travel back?" He exposed his vicious canine teeth. "I don't suppose you would be partial to me hurling you across the ocean, would you?"

Amaymon elbowed me gently. "Or I could just shove you in again."

"Fuck off," I replied as I picked up my gun and holstered it. Djinn rested comfortably in its sheath.

I turned to Jehudiel. "Think you could do me a favor?"

He nodded and laid his hand on my shoulder. All I heard was the gentle flapping of wings and the world spun as we disappeared.

Chapter 28

We appeared on the pier.

And by we, I mean Jehudiel and myself. The two demons travelled through portals. No self-respecting demon would be caught dead hitching a ride with an angel. That's how the end of the world starts.

"You took your time." Gil stood there leaning against a white, unmarked van. As if she wasn't creepy enough already.

"You weren't much help," I shot back. "How's the concussion?"

"I'm fine. Thank you, Erik." That sounded sincere enough.

"So, what do you want?" I asked.

Her face was an ice sculpture. "I need to determine whether you're a danger to society. I saw your change," she said. "That is a dangerous power. Mephisto tells me you wielded Life magic."

Figures. My sister never sends backup for free. There was

always a catch, always a price.

"And who gave you the authority to judge me?" I held out my hand before she could answer. "Yeah, let me guess, some secret society whose name you can't even utter out loud? Spooky."

Gil folded her arms and huffed. "This has nothing to do with that. This area is my responsibility and I don't want someone with your destructive record running around with powers that are beyond his control."

"I have plenty of control," I said.

"You destroy almost everything you touch," she rebutted.

"No, I don't."

And just as I said that, there was a loud crunch of metal. The tanker was a good distance from the pier but still visible. It was already battered, even before the battle that took place on it. The ship crunched and bent and actually folded down the middle before gently sinking amidst waves and white foam.

Great timing, universe.

"I… That…"

I saw Gil raise her eyes and heard Amaymon chuckle.

"Oh come on, that was an accident," I blurted out.

"Nice save, dude," muttered the demon.

"Shut up!"

Gil cleared her throat. "Current demonstrations not withstanding, you have powers that you do not understand," she said. "Can you guarantee that you won't go on any rampages?"

"How the hell should I know?" I yelled exasperatedly.

"You're the genius of the family. So, how about you tell me what the hell is going on with me?"

Amaymon let out a chuckle. "Heh. This is better than cable."

Gil's eyes narrowed dangerously. "Tell me all you know about your powers. When did you get them? Under which circumstances? I want to know everything," she said.

We glared at each other for a second.

Should I spill the beans here and now? I mean, if this was a family thing Gil had the right to know, but I wasn't sure I wanted Mephisto and Jehudiel to hear this. Who knows what I could reveal, or how they might use that against me. I might be giving them my Achilles Heel on a silver platter without even knowing it. And, trust me, you do not want to have your strings pulled by either one.

I weighed the pros and cons and felt my brain slowly starting to melt. Then, I made my decision the only way I know how.

"Ah, fuck it," I said before telling Gil everything.

"This is… unique."

Mistress of understatement. Gil must have noticed my expression because she folded her arms defensively.

"Although, admittedly, there's very little I know about this particular subject," she admitted.

"Lemme give you the cliff-notes version. I have a ton of magic I cannot use, because of a curse," I said, extending one finger. Then, I began counting off on the other fingers. "I can heal from almost anything due to my magic being trapped inside of me. Which means I am constantly charged with magic."

"A gross oversimplification, but go on," she interjected.

"Now, I find out I can use Life magic. I don't know how or why, but he says I can," I said, pointing at Jehudiel. "So, I'm gonna take his word for it. Oh, and let's not forget the anima particles he shoved inside me."

"That sounds kinda gross man," Amaymon quipped.

I ignored him. "Remember when Dad tried to kill us?"

Gil's eyes darkened. "How can I ever forget?"

"Our bloodline is cursed and he wanted to kill us to keep all that power for himself," I continued. "I guess it was only a matter of time before our inherited power manifested."

Mephisto cleared his throat. I didn't know dogs could do that. Then again, this was Mephisto we're talking about.

"If you remember our talk correctly, I explained how your bloodline curse sucks power from the current Head of Household and gives it to the next, with each having both their own power and that of their ancestors available to them. But when you two were born, that vast power was split in two. It was that trauma—as well as other circumstances of a more insidious nature—that changed your father into the man he became."

"You mean a killer who tried to sacrifice his own children?" I spat.

"Yes. Now that you have both matured enough, you will begin to access your powers." He turned his snout at my direction. "Your first experience with this power was when you forcefully claimed your portion to fight against your father."

I remembered being in that room, confronting my father. I remember him injecting himself with drugs to boost his powers. I remember the fighting. After that I blacked out and remember nothing. Only a vague memory, that of a tree in a red desert and a figure calling my name.

Offering me help—offering me power.

Then, I came to and found the lab in the mansion's basement destroyed and Dad in ruins. He was dying, and no drugs or magic could have changed that. I remembered Gil fainting and Mephisto telling me to run.

That night I had to run away, so that Gil could stay out of danger.

"Yeah. I remember," I said darkly. As you can imagine, this wasn't the most comfortable subject for me to talk about.

Mephisto kept going, completely oblivious to our feelings.

"And Master Gil came into her power shortly afterwards, when she killed your father-"

"Mephistopheles!" Gil's sudden outburst made all of us jump. Her eyes were wide with panic and her poker face completely shattered.

"Oh dear," Mephisto said, in the most insincere tone possible.

"You did what?" I blurted out.

I had killed our father. I did it, not Gil. I went all crazy and left him for dead. I had shouldered that fact for years, never once regretting it.

But it was my burden to carry, not Gil's.

She wouldn't meet my eyes.

"I killed Dad," I reaffirmed. "Right, Gil?"

She didn't answer me. She just kept staring at her shoes.

"No."

Her voice was barely a whisper. "You just left him for dead, but the concoction of drugs and magic he was under kept him alive. Barely, but alive." She actually started shaking.

"So, once you left, I grabbed a piece of glass and I-" There were tears in her eyes now, but she kept herself from breaking down. "I dragged it across his throat."

There was stunned silence.

It all made sense now. Her sense of duty, taking up the family business, trying to make it better and more humane but still keeping the Warlock traditions and practices alive. She was atoning for Dad's mistakes. For the mistakes all our ancestors, in fact.

For years I thought I was the one with the burden. Turns out my sister was making amends for our entire ancestry. I thought she had become a cold-hearted bitch.

Turns out she was the real hero after all.

And on that pier I did something I hadn't ever thought I'd do again: I hugged my sister. Not the leader of the Ashendale mansion or some businesswoman, but my real sister.

It was a brief hug, but it mattered. After all these years, after all we had been through, it took this moment of understanding to finally reconcile us.

"So, what now?" I asked, finally letting her go and backing away.

"The both of you need to awaken your powers, but even that might not be sufficient," Mephisto said. "You are two halves of a whole. From now on you must both act as one entity." He let out a laugh. "Personally, I would wager my money on the Sins right now."

That was the last straw. I was about to say something, but Gil beat me to the punch.

"Leave," she said in a tone that suggested pain.

"I'm sorry, Master. I apologize for speaking out of turn."

He wasn't and Gil knew it.

"Again," Amaymon added with utter glee.

"Leave," she repeated.

Mephisto turned tail and disappeared inside a portal.

Once he was gone, Gil turned to me. "He is right, though. We need to understand ourselves, what these new powers are, and do it fast."

"Do you already know what your power is?"

She blinked once, very deliberately. "No."

Even I knew that was a blatant lie.

"But you can come back home if you want," she said before I could say anything.

"Yeah," Amaymon said. "You guys should stick together for now. You only defeated Lilith 'cause her powers weren't complete. She wasn't fully in tune with the Sin of Lust and that made her fall to pieces." He chuckled at his own pun.

"But seriously," he went on. "The next Sin ain't gonna be so easy. Mephisto's right. You got no chance unless you stick together." He cracked his neck. "Besides, you ain't got no office. And a warm shower would be nice."

They were all valid points.

But I couldn't bring myself to leave that office. It symbolized my independence and my growth. I had literally constructed that dingy little hole from the ground up. It was my home in a way that the mansion never was.

"Thanks, but no thanks," I said. "We may be allies now but I still got a business to run. I'm not a Warlock, Gil."

She held her hand up. "I get it. Just promise me we'll work together, okay?"

I smiled. It was like catching a glimpse of the little girl I grew up with again.

"Sure thing. We'll stick together," I said. She nodding and turned to leave.

"Oh, Gil," I called out. "Wait."

She stopped behind the open limo door.

"When you were unconscious on the boat, I remember feeling something," I said. "My black shadow stuff reacted with your aura and there was something like… like fog or smoke."

Her face remained impassive.

"Was that your spell?" I insisted.

"Not that I recall," she replied shortly.

"How come you knew about these powers?" I asked. "Seems to me like you had a couple of hints. And if you knew what was gonna happen to me, you must have taken note of what was gonna happen to you. You know, since we're twins and all that."

"Is there a point you're trying to make, brother?"

"Yes," I said. "What are you hiding?"

I saw her shake her head a little. "You know, you're not as clueless as you seem," she muttered.

Maybe it was the sun, but I could swear her body shimmered in white fog for a second, like a thin breath in winter.

"I have no idea what you're talking about," she said, before winking and disappearing into the car.

Son of a…

"Hey, Gil," I called but it was too late. The car drove off, followed by the white van.

"Too late," Amaymon said.

"I know!" I retorted exasperatedly.

He grinned. "Think this is gonna come back to bite you in the ass?"

"You know it." I turned to where Jehudiel had stood quietly all this time, but saw nothing but empty space. "Hey, where'd he go?"

"He left a second ago," Amaymon replied.

Figures. He was done with his duty. From here on, we were on our own.

Amaymon and I started walking back towards the rental car.

"Back to the office it is, then," I said. "Whatever's left of it anyway."

He smirked. "Yep. Back to lickin' myself clean."

"Admit it, you love doing that."

"Yeah, but where'd you think I get hairballs from?"

"Ew."

Chapter 29

This was supposed to be a happy ending, where the hero gets a steamy kiss from the damsel in distress, answers to all the questions, and a new power and responsibility to contend with.

Hey, one out of three wasn't bad. I got the power, a crap load of new responsibility and even managed to get a hug.

When we came into her line of sight, Abigail wrapped her arms around me and started crying. I guess it was to be expected given the trauma she went through. Amaymon jumped out of the car in kitty form and she pressed him on her chest. He purred delightfully and she kissed his little feline head.

Lucky bastard.

I sighed and turned to receive my prize: a pile of rubble I once called home. After the hell I went through on this case, the last thing I wanted was to enter my office and be surrounded by more debris and destruction.

"No rest for the wicked," I murmured with a chuckle.

That was the same retort I shot at Lilith.

Guess the universe finally took a liking to my jokes.

I decided to procrastinate a little further by digging up my cell phone and calling Gracie Valdez. I mean, she did hire me after all, and I suppose both she and Abigail deserved a tearful reunion.

As if on cue, Gracie appeared out of thin air. "Abi!"

Wow. She did say she was an adept but I didn't think she was this good a clairvoyant. Almost immediately Abigail lunged at her, and a second later the two girls were busy exchanging hugs, tears and squeaks.

I stood back, giving the best friends some privacy, and sat down on the single stair on my porch and just stared at the ground.

Something was not right about that girl.

Gracie's shadow was out of proportion but it was not a trick of the sun. The sun doesn't make you look like an armored, six foot figure with large wings on your back.

"Ah, crap!"

It was more of a moan rather than a warning. I got up and went towards them. By now they were both staring at me as if I had snapped.

My hand reached for my short sword and I pulled out Djinn in a swift, well-practiced move. Not that I had the strength to fight an angel. The most I could do right now was distract him with some jumping jacks.

Maybe that would be enough to save the succubus.

"Mr. Ashendale, what is the meaning of-" Gracie began.

"Shut up," I snapped. "I know you're an angel."

Abigail gave me a bewildered look.

"The shadow," I said by way of an explanation.

She must have noticed because she sprung away from Valdez like a frightened cat.

"You're either ready to pounce and didn't bother with a good disguise," I said, "or you're just an idiot." Djinn quivered in my hand. "Either way, you're not getting the girl."

Gracie Valdez laughed. Her body began dissolving in a glow of light and in her place stood Jehudiel.

"Or, I could be making your life easier," he said in that melodic tone of his.

I pushed Djinn back into its sheath. "Unless a bunch of you angels are gonna put on hard hats and help out with that disaster," I said as I pointed at the remains of my office, "I don't see how much help you can be."

Jehudiel put on his helmet, which promptly changed into a hard hat. "I'll see what I can do," he said brightly.

He snapped his finger and there was an intense flash of light. The office began repairing itself. The holes in the wall filled up and the furniture went back to its proper place, fully repaired. Even the doorbell that Amaymon had bent out of shape was repaired. A familiar buzz of magic indicated that all the crystals were back in their position inside the walls, enabling my magic.

While I was busy fawning over my office, I heard Abigail sniff and turned just in time to watch her wipe away a tear.

"How?" she asked the archangel. Her expression morphed into a feral scowl. "Did she ever exist?" she demanded. "Was my best friend just an illusion? Did I imagine it all, all those years of being together with her?"

Jehudiel nodded slowly, before bending over into a deep bow. "Yes," he replied. "They were all fake memories which I planted. I am so sorry. I had to gain your trust early on, and keeping secrets from me would have hastened your death. I hope you can forgive me."

I wasn't sure what her forgiveness method was until Abigail stepped forwards and slapped the angel in the face.

"Never do that again," she said angrily. "Don't ever mess with my head again. Ever, you hear me?"

Jehudiel remained silent. Abigail gave him one last glare before pushing past me and going inside the office.

"Point, redhead," Amaymon muttered.

Jehudiel ignored him and entered the office too.

Okay then, apparently everyone was invited.

Once inside the archangel smiled at us. "Heaven thanks you for your service," he announced.

Then he waved his hand and, like a scene from *Fantasia,* a silver tray with burgers and cakes appeared on the coffee table. On my desk table, stacks of paper money were piled up on top of each other—more money than I had ever seen in my entire life.

Certainly more than enough to buy each of us an office and maybe a mansion to go with it.

"We take care of our own," Jehudiel said as he beamed at each of us. Abigail just glared at the empty space around the angel while Amaymon flicked his tail and muttered something obscene.

I just put on my best poker face. "You take care of your own?"

"Yes."

"And since when am I 'one of your own'?" I quoted.

Jehudiel's eyes remained blank. Not that he ever wore an expression to begin with, but he was usually more human than the others. Now, he had reverted back to his Terminator face. "You and your sister have pledged your services to Heaven's forces. Please, wait for our call."

There was a moment of silence as I digested that piece of information and read in between the lines.

Then, I punched the angel in the face.

Jehudiel reeled back. Something about his stumble seemed so fake, so unnatural. He let me hit him—of course he let me hit him. I was nowhere near strong enough to actually touch the angel, let alone deck him. And if I hadn't been busy yelling at him, I would have stopped to question why he had let me punch him in the face.

"Are you fucking kidding me?" I yelled. I looked around to see both Abigail and Amaymon utterly speechless.

"Pledged our services?" I continued. "Who the fuck are you to say that? When did I pledge my services? I took your case as a human, not as an angel. You wanna go off and fight for eternity in an impossible battle, go ahead. Just leave Earth out of it."

"Your sister-" he began.

"My sister's decisions do not include me," I shot back. "We may be twins, we may have the same inherited power, be two halves of a whole and all that, but we *are not* the same person. Her decisions are hers, and hers alone."

Jehudiel's wings flared an inch. Amaymon was instantly in human form, ready to pounce. I held my hand up, stopping him.

"I'm not saying I will not take the case," I told the archangel. He relaxed an inch. "But I'm doing it for people like her," I said pointing at Abigail, who was still rooted on the couch. "People who are in danger and helpless against whatever is tormenting them."

I took a breath to calm myself down. *Don't blow this now, Erik.*

"If a Sin makes it to Earth and you guys want my help, then call me. Otherwise, go whine to my sister," I said. "If there are people in need, I will help, but in my way. But keep this plane away from your war, or I will become your enemy."

I leaned in very close. "And we both know I'm the last person you folks want as your enemy right now."

That hit home.

Jehudiel's wings flared and he bathed the office in light.

"I am Jehudiel, Archangel and Virtue." His voice shook every molecule in my body. "If you hinder our holy war you will be smitten."

I remained unfazed. I mean, come on; I died, went to a pocket dimension, came back supercharged, died again and was saved, only to defeat a giant demonic progenitor using a unique combination of angelic and supercharged wizard magic. If he wanted to intimidate me, this guy was going to have to seriously up his game.

"And I am Erik Ashendale, Wizard and Owner of Demonic Cat," I retorted. "I'm the only guy you assholes can depend on. So how about we stop this charade?"

The archangel and I were now locked in a staring contest. A very stressful staring contest.

"You'd do well to remember, mortal," he finally said, "that while we do need you, you are not indispensable."

His incandescent wings flapped once and Jehudiel disappeared from sight. Nice way to get the last word in, I suppose.

"You have a nice day, too," I yelled. "Asshole."

"He can't hear you, Erik," Amaymon interjected as he wolfed down two burgers at once.

"Whatever." I grabbed some food. "Fairy looking douche bag."

"I know, right?" Abigail said. "I'm glad you stood up to him, Erik. Even though that guy is scary powerful."

"Nah, I could've probably taken him," Amaymon said.

"Sure you could," I said condescendingly.

I started to count the money Jehudiel made appear on my desk and found a small envelope on top of the pile. I tore it open and a sharp piece of iron fell into my palm. It felt somewhat familiar. Inside the envelope I also found a Post-It note with a street address on it and sighed.

That angel knew all along that I would want to do things my way. He set up the whole thing so that I would assemble my own ragtag team.

But did I really want this particular guy on my team?

I shook my head. I would have ended up exactly like him,

lost and in trouble, if my mentor hadn't found me. Guess now it was my turn to return that kindness.

I walked towards the front door.

"Going somewhere?" Abigail asked.

"Yeah," I said. I looked at the coat and decided against it. It was too hot anyway. Let the people stare: I was done trying to please everyone. I was doing the right thing and that was all that mattered.

"I got a loose end to tie up."

***

Jack the elemental was flung from across the street into an alleyway. This wasn't the most reputable part of town, which meant no one came here unless they had to.

The angel's directions had led me here, and all the confirmation I needed that I was in the right place was seeing the metal elemental going airborne and land on a pile of trash.

"Jack, Jack, Jack," I said as I emerged from behind a corner and helped him up. "Always in a pile of crap."

He looked at me with doe eyes. "Aren't you that wizard?"

"No, I'm the Tooth Fairy, but I left my skirt at home," I shot back sarcastically.

Jack rolled his eyes.

"What happened?" I asked.

"Them," he answered, pointing forwards.

I followed his finger and saw a trio of hulking thugs walking up to us carrying batons.

"Three jokers with sticks?" I asked him. "That's your trouble?"

"Hey, you. Nerd," called out the first one. "Get away from that guy unless you wanna get pummeled."

Electricity crackled threateningly from his baton.

"Oh. Cattle prods," I said, completely ignoring them, and talking to Jack. "That would nullify your metal." Then I turned to them. "Hey, that's my trick. Get your own method."

They had no idea what I was talking about, of course.

"So, let me guess," I said. "You owe these assholes some money."

Jack nodded. "Their boss."

"Figures. They look too dumb to count."

I took out a roll of bills and chucked it at one of them. "Take that to your boss and disappear," I said.

The lead gorilla's eyes squinted. "We still wanna beat this guy up. He's some kinda freak."

I extracted Djinn. "Fuck off."

But I knew they weren't going to fuck off. In fact they did just the opposite and charged at me.

One of them dove towards Jack and the two struggled with each other.

The other two whipped their prods at me. Here's the thing: I don't use magic against regular people. In my mind it just isn't fair. And having fought asmodaii, demons, and all sorts of monsters, these guys weren't even a quarter of the challenge.

My sword sliced through the cattle prod and I lashed out with my leg. I caught the guy squarely in the chest and he dropped like a stone, wheezing and hacking on the ground.

The other grabbed my neck. I blocked, kicked him in the groin and smashed Djinn's pommel on his head.

Game over.

Meanwhile, Jack and asshole number three were still tussling with each other. I rolled my eyes. These guys were supposed to be thugs. The least you would expect was for them to have some knowledge of fighting.

I lifted my leg and brought the heel down on the thug's shoulder. I heard a bone snap as the guy gasped. He fell down, moaning and writhing in pain. My leg felt funny. I saw shadows drifting off and the sole of my boot flapping.

Great.

My powers were going haywire again thanks to that boost I received on the ship. I guess that's the price you pay for superpowers these days. This meant I had to retrain myself from stage one again. Maybe that was why Jehudiel wanted me to take Jack under my wing. If I trained him from scratch, I would be retraining myself in the basics as well.

I helped Jack up. "Come on. You owe me a new pair of boots by the way."

Chapter 30

Jack let out a whistle as we both entered my office. "Damn, you must have one hell of a cleaning crew," he muttered.

I headed straight for the kitchen. "Make yourself comfortable," I called out as I looked for some soda. I returned with two cans only to find him at my drawer, toying around with something metallic.

"Were you ever going to use these again?" he asked.

He held up a broken gun slide, the remains of one of the guns I had destroyed years ago. I didn't have the heart to return it back to Bobby.

"Nah, those are busted," I replied.

"No, I can fix this no problem," he said with a frown. He rummaged inside the box and mumbled to himself. I felt him use trace amounts of his powers, manipulating the metal on a molecular level.

"There, it's done," he said handing me the gun.

I put my soda can down and checked the weapon. It was fully functional with all the nuts and bolts working perfectly.

"How did you do that?"

"Figured it's the least I can do after I busted up your office and all that." He shrugged. "I'm good with metal. I guess this power is good for something."

That gave me an idea. I motioned for him to sit down and offered him a soda.

"How would you like a job?" I asked.

He cocked an eyebrow. "You want me to repair every gun you break?"

"No," I said. "But I know a guy who's a blacksmith and he's getting too old for it. He's always whining about wanting an apprentice to carry on the shop. Sounds like something you would be good at."

"As long as it's metal, I'm good with it," he replied.

I believed him. I've seen him in action. He only lost to me because he didn't know how to use his powers, and had the strategic mind of a duck. But with some training he could be something.

"Anything to get off the streets," he added. "But I want to know more about myself. What my powers are, how to use them, that sort of thing. The stuff only you can help me with."

I smiled. "Sure thing."

We bumped cans and sealed the deal.

"Hey, what about me?" Abigail came down the stairs, followed by Amaymon in cat form.

"Succubii don't use magic," I said.

She beamed at the cat. "Do you want to tell him or shall I?"

"Tell me what?" I asked.

Amaymon cleared his throat and sat on top of the banister so all of us had to look up to him. He must have loved that.

"A succubus does not have magic, this is true," he said. "However, Abigail is still a human, technically speaking. She has a Core, the source of magic which all humans have. When she becomes a succubus this Core usually dies out and it's bye bye magic. But not in this case."

He paused and looked at the three of us. "Usually it takes a strong magical boost or trauma to forcefully awaken someone's Core. That what happened to Abigail when she was attacked."

"But she's already got the succubus DNA in her," I said.

"That is true. But Lilith awakened her Core—her *human* Core—which means that now Abigail can use magic. I'm not sure what is gonna happen next year when she comes of age. If that happens at all."

"What do you mean?" I asked.

"Abigail is the first ever witch-succubus hybrid," replied the feline. "On one hand, she could lose her magic and become a full succubus. However, and this is more likely, she may never actually become a succubus. She would still have the hunger and the power, just not on that level. She most likely won't need to kill. However, this possibility is only certain if she uses her magical powers—her *human* magical powers—as much as she can."

Abigail was actually vibrating as she beamed at me. "Which means that I have to learn magic. And use it. Like, a lot."

Jack sprang from his seat. "Hi, I'm Jack," he said beaming.

Oh, the poor, smitten bastard.

She shook his hand. "You a wizard?"

"Elemental," Amaymon supplied.

"I can manipulate metal," Jack added.

"Oh, cool, show me."

I grabbed Jack's shoulder. "You guys can play with each other later."

"She's way outta your league, bro," said the cat. "Although you guys make for an interesting love triangle."

"Shut up," I said.

The cat ignored me. "I mean, I can see Erik and Abigail humpin' off, but Jack must have one solid rod. Get it? 'Cause he's a metal elemental."

"Shut up, Amaymon, or I'm getting a pet coyote," I said dragging Jack away.

"You were right," I heard Abigail whisper to the cat. "It is easy to mess with him."

And that was that.

Twice a week Jack would come over for basic training, along with Abigail. The poor kid really was out of his league, but hey, she *was* a succubus. Driving men out of their mind with lust is what they do.

And speaking of driving men out of their mind, Abigail had managed to get herself a job as my secretary.

No, I don't know how it happened.

Yes, Amaymon was involved.

As he had so tactfully pointed out, I had no idea how to

do my accounts, and had the manners of a caveman. A hot babe—as Amaymon kept referring to her—would apparently make clients feel better. She was good for business. Again, his words not mine.

What's more, he offered her the spare bedroom upstairs until she could get an apartment of her own. She wasn't going back to college and instead settled for evening classes and online education. She wanted to focus on her powers first. That was when the cat had become very generous.

Who are we kidding? That pervert is never letting the hot secretary leave.

There was also some discussion over how competent a teacher I can be.

"Don't screw 'em up," Amaymon had said.

"I can teach them!" I had retorted.

"Sure you can," he replied condescendingly.

"Put a sock in it, Captain Negative."

"Aye, aye, Sergeant Deluded."

"One more comment outta you and no more belly rubs."

"Please, teach us, O Enlightened One."

That ended that argument once and for all.

The three of us sat on the floor, with the cat prowling around us. The couches and coffee table had been pushed aside, giving us an open area. We started off with some mediation to strengthen their flow of energy.

"Oum." Amaymon occasionally oversaw our lessons and made it his mission to interrupt at every possible second.

"Oum." He made a really wet hacking noise. "Fucking hairball."

There was only reason I tolerated him. If they could concentrate through his crap they would learn faster, and be better prepared for the real world, where there were plenty of distractions everywhere.

Then, halfway through the lesson, the phone rang.

"I hear bells. Am I in Nirvana?" asked the cat. He looked around. "Nope. Still in this shit hole."

I ignored him as the others just laughed and answered the phone. "What?"

"See why you're needed?" Amaymon whispered to Abigail. "He's got the manners of a water buffalo."

"Erik, it's Roland." I waved them silent so I could listen to the cop.

"I'll be there soon," I said and put the receiver down, before turning my attention back to my students. "There's a couple of poltergeists scaring off mourners at the cemetery. It shouldn't take long."

Poltergeists weren't dangerous—annoying as hell, though. I grabbed my stuff and turned to see my two students staring at me like I was Santa Clause and had skipped their names on the list.

Like I said, poltergeists aren't dangerous. They might even make a good training exercise.

"You follow my every order to the letter, got it?" I said as I waved a finger at them.

They nodded fervently.

"Fine. Come along," I said with resignation. "Amaymon,

you come as well. In case it gets too out of hand."

"What's in it for me?"

I smirked. "I'll make sure Abigail never gives you another belly rub. Ever," I added threateningly.

He immediately stood up on all fours. "Your orders, Sir?"

A few days ago I had found Amaymon's weak spot and was having the time of my life making him do what I wanted.

I watched my team get ready and we headed for the door. It felt good, having people to rely on, having friends. It felt like my little world was growing and, for once, it was all going to be just fine. As long as we stick together, nothing could take us down. I had allies and friends, and for the very first time in my life, I had family. And I knew they all had my back.

Something told me I would need the help of each and every one of them. We only won this round by sheer luck, a bug in Lilith's system. Both Amaymon and Mephisto made it clear that a fully powered Sin would be much tougher.

Tougher than any of us, actually.

So we had to be ready for the next one. And the one after that. Until the world can breathe safely again. This is our world, our home, and it's up to us to protect it. That's our job, our calling. We'll keep everyone safe, sometimes for a fee. Wizards need to eat, as well.

But we always do the right thing, for the right reasons. Of that, I was sure.

I smiled.

Okay, universe. Whatever you got in store for us next, bring it on.

We're ready.

READY FOR MORE?

You've reached the end of this story but Erik's adventure isn't over yet. Check out *Birthright*, Book 2 of the *Legacy* series.

BOOK 2: BIRTHRIGHT

BOOK 3: LOST ONES

Join the *Legacy* world

Check out the link below and subscribe to the author's mailing list for some freebies and updates.

http://ryanattard.com

You can also contribute by leaving a review online - even a few words would suffice.
Any praise or support is greatly appreciated.

Thank you for reading.

You might also enjoy my other series *The Pandora Chronicles*.

THE PANDORA CHRONICLES
BOOK 1

ABOUT THE AUTHOR

Ryan Attard is the author of the *Legacy* series, *The Pandora Chronicles* and, as of recently, *Evil Plan Inc.* When not tormenting his protagonists or ruling over his imaginary worlds, Ryan can be found within the confines of his house on an island far, far away, either geeking out about the latest manga chapter he read, or the television show he just watched.

Or he could be found spewing his opinions and telling jokes on his weekly podcast, *The Lurking Voice Podcast*, which can be found through his website (although if you are easily offended you should definitely not listen).

He is also the kind of person who writes about himself in the third person.

Email at ryanattardauthor@gmail.com
Website: http://ryanattard.com
Twitter: https://twitter.com/Enkousama

Printed in Great Britain
by Amazon